Toxic

Bernard Smith

Contents

The golden duo

Mariah turned around as she felt a hand along over her shoulder. She shivered when she saw his face.

"Turn around" He said and Mariah did as she was told. She took a deep breath in as they walked towards the school gates.

Students were piling up at the assembly ground already. A lot of them smiled at her. A few waved. Everyone in school knew her, everyone. That presented a problem in itself albeit the least of her worries, she hated that in a school of not less that 600 students, she was the most popular. It wasn't in her nature to go seeking for attention, attention came looking for her. She was beautiful, she knew it and when she had first arrived at Cedar Court High School, she'd been told that there was an ongoing bet on who would succeed in taking her out. JJ won that bet. Didi she regret going out with JJ?

A little.

"Hey" he said squeezing her shoulder, "see you later"

Clearing her throat a little, she nodded and he left. JJ was always slinging his guitar on his shoulder, he loved that thing, maybe even more than her.

Shaking her head she walked to where her class was standing and joined the back of the line.

Students stood by class. Mariah was in the advanced classes and JJ wasn't so they never stood together.

Mariah always felt that she wasn't the type of girl boys liked. Sure she was beautiful, but she was nerdy and she always felt herself to be quite awkward. But then she went through puberty and then she grew curves, and everything guys admired.

She droned out the voice of the vice principal as she let her thought wander off. He was saying the usual boring stuff, first day of the week, be good... Don't loiter... Blah blah blah.

Her eyes wandered into the crowd. A pair of eyes on the boys line caught her attention. He had his hands in his pocket and he had his right foot in front of his left as he rested his weight on his right leg. He was looking at her but he wasn't staring. It didn't look like he knew her, like he was trying to figure out something from her face.

Kami tapped her shoulder"That's the new guy" she said excitedly

"He's already eyeing Mariah, na wa o" Rebekah said dropping behind her.

Mariah rolled her eyes. Girls were jealous of her, she was used to it. She didn't understand why? Because she was smart? Or because she was dating JJ?

"He's rich" Kami continued, paying no attention whatsoever to Rebekah.

Mariah rolled her eyes again, "Like I care" she said to Kami, "How do you know sef?

"He came with military men as escorts" Kami said in a duh tone

"Well, how was I supposed to know that?" Mariah forced herself to say.

"How would you know? When you're always so busy with him" Kami said pointing to JJ's side of the line. As if on cue he glanced at them and looked away. Then he looked back at her and fixed his gaze on her. He was telling her something. She had learnt to read his facial expressions early on in their relationship. She quickly turned away. She could feel JJ's eyes boring holes into her head.

"I hope he isn't in our class" Mariah said quietly.

"I hope he is" Kami said, "Then I'll get to talk to him and maybe he'd be my first boyfriend. You never know"

Mariah chuckled. Kamikaze was class president, which meant that she got to speak to all new students before anyone else all while claiming to be 'doing her job'"That should be a crime of some sort. Using your power as an unfair advantage"

Kami shrugged just as the whispers go louder at the assembly ground.

"What's going on?" Mariah asked Kami. They both hadn't been listening, so none of them could tell what the Vice Principal had been talking about. Kami took a few steps forward as she listened to the conversations of the girls in front of them.

"It's a science competition. We'll take an exam to chose the top three. 'A' classes only. The exam is today"

"Okay" Mariah said half heartedly. She and Kami were in the 'A' class. They advanced class. Where the teachers speak a thousand words per minute and they covered the syllabus in a month and they were all on fast track to the university even at age 15.

The students were dismissed and Kami headed up to the principal's office with their teacher to get the exam questions.

Mariah made her way to her seat by the window facing the street. She hung her bag on the handle of her chair as she settled into her seat.

Kami came in moments later with test questions and Mr new guy behind her. Mr Micah, their class teacher followed closely behind. The students quickly made it to their seats.Mr Micah cleared his throat.

"Are you all here?" He asked

"Yes sir" they chorused

"I would take a roll call but I don't care. It's not like any of you stand a chance if passing this test anyways" Mr Micah said. Mariah chuckled. Was she nervous? Heck no! Mariah never failed. That's not pride, that's a fact. Mr Micah was not necessarily mean, he just couldn't be bother by a lot of things and he hated dummies or as he exquisitely called them, 'olodos'

"We have a new student with us today. This guy." he said pointing at the new guy. "decided to show up two weeks after the term had begun. Pretty stupid if you ask me" the class chuckled, "So tell us your name... "

"My na..." new guy began

"Shut up" Mr Micah said shushing him. "I didn't ask you anything"

Mariah chuckled. What a bad day to start school. First the test and now Mr Micah.

New guy smiled and nodded. He wasn't fazed by Micah at all

"Tell them your name, your previous school and your score on the entrance exam"

New guy remained silent, staring at Mr Micah, "Go on, talk" Micah urged him. "My name is Harrison Akpojevwe. I moved here from owerri, from Command secondary school. I scored a 96.8 in the test"

Gasps and whispers were heard through out the room.

"He almost beat Mariah's high score"

"He's freaking smart"

Mariah rolled her eyes. Sure the guy had a 96.8. But she had scored a 97 the highest score in Cedar Court's history of entrance exams.This Harrison guy, was not all that.

"Enough." Mr Micah said, he nodded to Kami who started distributing the test questions, he pointed to an empty seat and Harrison took his seat. "Let's see how stupid you actually are. This test is probably the hardest you'd ever write. Try not to fail"

Mariah flipped the script over as soon as Kami dropped it on her desk, she carefully wrote her name and number on the dotted lines left for that purpose.

"fifty questions, forty-five minutes" Mr Micah said when Kami had gotten to her seat beside Mariah. "Start now" The room was silent only the sound of pages flipping through out the room and pencils shading the right answer. "If you do not know how to solve number one, you might as well give up now. Number two is not going to be any better"

Mariah rolled her eyes. Number one. She read the question, particle distribution theory. Pfft. Easy.

A little antsy

Mariah couldn't sit still. She was waiting for the bell. The bell signifying that it was lunch time. Then Mr Micah would come in with the score as and she'd be put out of this misery she'd put herself into. She was never nervous. She never felt nervous. Especially after a test, because she never failed but this time she felt like she had something to prove. Maybe to herself, she didn't know.

Suddenly the bell rang startling her and almost sending her out of her seat. As if on cue Mr Micah walked in with the score sheet in his left hand and his right hand in his pocket.

"Shut up. And sit down, empty vessels" he said. The class complied as the noise slowly died down. "Straight to the point, y'all failed this test. Not a single person got all the questions right. I am very disappointed. You don't deserve lunch. But what's my business right? It's not my name you're disgracing nor is it my money you are wasting paying for an education. Anyways" he said moving to rest his weight on the desk in front of him, "From the bottom to the top shall we? Akorah, Myrrh. You had 30 over fifty. Ekwere, Diamond, 30 over fifty. Akpobaro, Onoride, 31 over fifty..."

Mariah groaned as she placed her hand on her desk reminding herself to start listening when he got to the forty's.

"... Oreva, Everistus 42 over fifty, Ubah, Ivan 43 over fifty. Chuks, Chimezie, 43 over fifty... "

Mariah was holding her breath. Her class had thirty people and he'd called out 26 names already, only 4 people were left.

"... Okojie, Rebekah 45 over 50."

Mariah's heart was pounding. Why are you nervous. You're the best. She was telling herself all while tapping her fingers continuously on her desk.

"...Abraham, Kamseobong 46 over fifty"

Kami? Kami was usually number 2. Just her and Mr new guy left. If she lost to Mr new guy her pride would be wounded forever. After what seemed like ages Mr Micah finally continued

"... Akpojevwe, Harrison 47 over 50."

Mariah heaved a sigh of relief

"And finally, Caiaphas, Mariah 49 over fifty"

She smiled back at Kami who was smiling at her. "Caiaphas, Abraham and New guy... What's your name?" he said looking back at the score sheet.

"Akpojevwe..."

"Yes you. Whatever your name is. See me in the library during Study hall today, okay?"

"Yes sir" Harrison said and the girls nodded.

"Dismissed" Mr Micah said with a wave of his hand as he turned and left the class.

Noise erupted in the classroom again as students shuffled out of the doors to the refectory. Kami had class president privileges so they never rushed for food. It was always kept for them and they had a special table too. So they never rushed.

"Sorry. Excuse me" Mariah recognized his voice almost immediately. The new guy.

"Yeah. Hi" Kami said waving him over.

Mariah tried to resist rolling her eyes. Why were they all drooling over him. Sure he was tall and he had a nice smile and his eyes did that twinkling thing when he smiled...

Jesus. Mariah stop. She chided herself

He held the two desk in front of him and swung his legs over the seat very swiftly and very efficiently

"Hey. Sorry to bother. I'm new and I don't really know anyone except... You guys... And..."

"Oh sure it's no problem. We can show you around. I mean it's kind of my job anyways. I'm Kami, class president. This is my best friend Mariah" she said eyeing Mariah

Mariah rolled her eyes. "Nice to meet you" she said forcing a smile.

"Ah" he nodded, "Caiaphas. The smart one"

Mariah cocked one of her eyebrows up. "What's that supposed to mean?"

"Nothing." He shook his head, "You look more like a slay queen than a bookworm."

"well now I'm curious. What does a bookworm look like?" she asked him

Kami was stucknstaring between the two of them. Mariah was known to protect her position in class all the time. Who wouldn't? The worst thing that could ever happen to you was letting a newbie take your well deserved title away from you even if that newbie was fine and had beautiful eyes.

Kami shook her head as if to clear her thoughts.

"Look, I didn't mean to offend you, I just... You know what? I'm sorry. Forget I said that. Any of that"

Kami turned to her friend. Mariah was glaring at him.

"Okay. Let's go for lunch" she said as she led the way out of the classroom.

"Yeah. Where?" he asked her

"The refectory" kami said simply

Mariah followed silently behind them as Kami pointed out everywhere that mattered to the new guy. Library, staff room, staff cafeteria, principal's office, vice principal's office...Mariah didn't care and it took all the will in her body not to blurt it out in front of his face. She hated him. Why? Hell if she knew.

They got to the refectory several minutes later and a tired Mariah stepped into the hall.

"Food looks better that it did at command" New guy said

"Really? We complain about it a lot" Kami said as they weaved through the line of people waiting to be served heading to the front of the line

"What? Y'all should be grateful," new guy said, "This is real food, good food. In command 90% of the meal is water"

Kami chuckled and Mariah couldn't help smile. She realized all too quickly and her face was back to it's bored expression. God forbid he saw that she laughed at a joke he'd made. Almost laughed. Almost. They got to the front of the line and Mariah could see JJ's eyes looking right at her. He wasn't smiling. He'd been playing his guitar, she noticed. But he'd stopped. He guitar was still resting on his thigh. His left leg resting on the table and the rest of us body was on the window pane. His red guitar pick was still in his had and he was twirling it between his thumb and index finger. He didn't move an inch it was like he was on pause.

Kami handed a plate to her and another to New guy and she turned back to get hers

"Aren't we cutting lines right now? Isn't that a bad thing?" he whispered in her ear.

Mariah stilled. Wishing that this boy would stop talking to her. Or that JJ would suddenly turn blind.

"You know I know you don't like me. Which is really weird because people like me. Always... " he continued whispering to her.

"Stop talking to me" she said quietly, "Please"

Her eyes watched JJ carefully. He dropped his guitar on the table. Mariah swore he loved the guitar more than he loved her. In seconds he was beside her grabbing her wrist and glaring at new guy so viciously that Mariah was almost sure he would hit him.

In the next few seconds a series of events occurred. He pulled her wrist so hard the metal clasp of her watch bit into her skin. Causing her to drop her plate in pain. The plate landed on the floor with a loud clang, it's contents spilling all over the floor and breaking in two. He dragged her out of the refectory not caring where the whole school was watching them or not. Kami arrived the scene seconds later.

"What happened?" she asked Harrison her eyes darting between the floor and himself.

"I don't know. I was talking to her and some guy came and pulled her away" he said confused.

"Was it JJ?" she asked him forgetting for a second that he had just started at the school that day, "Describe him"

"Short. Not too short. Shorter than me. Dark. Red guitar pick in his hand" Harrison said

"Well, shit" was all Kami could muster. Harrison's brows furrowed in confusion.

Silence that knows

- -

"**A**re you crazy?" He seethed.

"JJ. What are you talking about?" She asked wriggling out of his grasp

"Why was he holding your hand? Why was he speaking in your ear? We're you trying to make me jealous? On purpose?"

"What are you talking about? He wasn't holding my hand"

"Are you calling me a liar?"

"JJ. I love you" Mariah said

"Really?"

"Yes. JJ. I wasn't holding his hand and he was only asking me why we were cutting the line. He's new, Mr Micah asked me and Kami to show him around" she lied through her teeth.

"Are you telling me the truth?" he asked her.

"Yes"

"OK. I'm sorry for yelling at you."

She nodded. She was struggling to maintain her breathing. Do not hyperventilate. Do not hyperventilate. She told herself.

"I wrote a new song, want to hear it?"

"Okay baby. I'll listen to it." she replied

He began to climb the steps. "Are you coming?" he asked when he saw she didn't budge.

"Yes. I just want to ease myself. I'll be up soon"

"Ok" he smiled. She smiled back at him and ran into the bathroom. The bathroom behind the refectory was shared for both sexes. There were kind of an after thought. Very small, only two stalls, one for boys and the other for girls, a mirror and sink in front of each stall and a hand dryer by the side. She leaned on one of the sinks her breathing quickened as she held her chest. Her head was spinning and she felt dizzy. "Oh God" she was mumbling over and over again. She heard the door open. She heard footsteps. She hoped it was Kami, she couldn't see. Her vision was blurry.

"Caiaphas" she heard.

Strong arms wrapped around her as she struggled to regularise her breathing.

"Relax... Relax..." the voice was saying.

"Count your breaths...one... Two.... Three"

Slowly, her breathing was going back to normal and her vision was clearing.She looked up at the person holding her.

"Harrison" she coughed out

"Yeah" he said awkwardly scratching his head. "Don't freak out" he said holding out his hands.In a flash she was in his arms crying. Bawling. He placed his hand on her back as he gently soothed her. The metal contraption that served as the tissue paper holder, stuck out of the wall his back was pressed against. Hurting him, he stayed still letting her cry her heart out, soaking his shift in the process. She was tall for a girl, he would say but she barely got up to his shoulder when he was at his full height. Her reddish brown hair stopped just about where the pockets in a dress shirt would normally be.

After a few minutes she lifted up, her head slowly.

"How are you?" he asked handing her a couple of tissues and finally moving away from the metal pressing into his back.

Mariah shrugged. "Why are you here?"

"To use the bathroom. Is he your boyfriend?"

She nodded

"Then why are you scared of him?"

"Stop it" she said walking past him

"Hold on." he pulled her back, "I'm sorry. I can never get it right with you can I?"

She chuckled, wiping her face again. "I need to go up there" she said pointing to the door.

"For what it's worth I don't think you should be scared of your own boyfriend. I know you probably don't need my opinion, but I'm just trying to be a friend."

He expected Mariah to breeze past him. Or even scream at him, tell him to mind his business but he was surprised when she smiled. "Thank you" she said.

It was genuine. It sounded genuine. He'd only met her today but he knew enough to know that she didn't deserve her controlling jerk of her boyfriend who gave her panic attacks.

She was pretty, very pretty and she was smart too. That he admired. Her brain. And at the risk of sounding weirdly obsessive he wanted them to be friends. He wanted her to like him.

He chuckled as he kicked open the door of the boys stall with his hands"Who cares if she likes me or not? Ugh. Who am I kidding, I care"

Mariah got upstairs to see that JJ had resumed plucking his guitar strings like nothing had happened. She heard a sigh of relief when she saw that no one was staring at her weirdly. They were just going about their normal businesses. She made her way slowly to her table. She took a seat beside Kami.

"I got you another plate" Kami whispered.

"I'm not hungry" she replied with a smile, "Maybe you can give it to one of the boys"

Kami rested her elbow on the table, perfectly blocking JJ from her line of sight."You always do this when you guys fight. You have to eat"

Mariah shook her head, "I'm fine. I'm serious"

Kai nodded as she sat up straight.

Harrison had taken a chair oppsite hers and Kami's. The table was a rectangular one, four people on each side, length wise and one at the head of the table, namely JJ. The only other side was empty seeing as it faced the passageway and putting a chair there would only disrupt the flow of traffic in the room.

In all honesty, Mariah didn't even think anyone was supposed to be sitting at the head of the tables as most of the other tables in the dining hall were pushed against the wall. But JJ was never one to care about rules, he did whatever he liked. He claimed rules did something bad to his artistic vibe, and whatnot.

Mariah's eyes met JJ's and he didn't say a word to her. He just looked away and continued plucking the strings of his guitar, one foot on the table and the other on the slab things that connected the two legs of the table to each other. Suddenly he jumped down from the window, pulled a chair as sat down.

"You guys are perfect you know that" Rebekah said.

"I know right? so perfect" Kami conccured. Sitting in between thee girls was always challenge, staying beside them in line was always a challenge. Anything that had to do with them would always present a challenge.

They hated each other. Mutually hated each other. They never agreed on anything except on rare occasions like the one she was currently witnessing. She'd always that they were exactly the same person, loud mouths, no filter, annoying but extremely nice people, the most loyal friends you could ask for.

"I'm literally doing nothing" Mariah replied

"Don't think we don't notice those sexy stares from across the table" Rebekah said.

Out of the corner of her eye she noticed Harrison was staring at her. Like really staring. It was like he was trying to read something from her face.

There was a plate of food in front of him but he wasn't eating it. His fork just moved the food on his plate around.

Mariah silently wished she could tell what he was thinking.

Harrison stared at her continuously. He knew she could tell, that he'd been looking at her for a while, but he just couldn't understand.

How could she be so sad and yet no one could see it? It was painfully obvious that she was merely existing, she did put up a great facade. Perfect grades, prefect hair, perfect body, perfect boyfriend...He scoffed. Perfect my foot

She had caught him staring at her severally but for some reason this time her gaze lingered on him. He gestured to her and tilted his head to the right, his lip upturned and his brows slightly raised he shrugged.She smiled. A small smile. The corners of her lips just turned up slightly. A barely there smile. Their exchange was silent, but it was genuine.A knowing silence.

Krazy Kami

B eing sexy is hard.

Hopeless.

Kami huffed as she crossed her legs at her knees, her perfectly pleated skirt riding up her legs.

God know how Mariah does it. Sexy is exhausting.

She had deviced a foolproof plan to get Harrison and here he was like every other guy in Cedarville smitten by her best friend.

Granted it was only his first day here but he hadn't even looked at her more than once.

They were currently in Mr Micah's office... Which was beside the physics laboratory, and they were supposed to be revising for the competition coming up in two weeks, but Kami was not concentrating at all.

Mr Micah was currently solving a problem on the white board in his office which also happened to be a map of Nigeria on the other side.

Her eyes followed Harrison's line of sight, he was staring at her best friend. Kami internally groaned. Mariah had no clue that this guy was staring at her, she was busy writing lazily in her notebook. Kami glanced at Harrison's page. He'd barely written anything past today's date and Mr Micah's name.

Turning to face them, Mr Micah capped his pen.

This caused Harrison to jerk. His head up and finally, finally stare at the board.

"Whew" he breathed out. He hadn't seemed to notice the board since he got there and he was stunned.

Mr Micah walked to his desk and began silently flipping over the text book on his desk.

"Excuse me sir" Harrison piped up. All three eyes were on him now. Harrison was not a fool, he'd known this school would test his limits before he came here, so he mentally prepared. Or he thought he did. What he didn't expect was being asked to cram months of teaching into two weeks. It was just outrageous and it seemed like he was the only one in the room who thought so.

"What competition is this for?" he asked no one in particular.

"The science Olympiad organized by STAN (Science Teachers Association of Nigeria). Last year we represented the state in the National level. We lost to Abuja by like three points" he continued

"Two" Mariah said simply. Avoiding everyone's gaze and still doodling on her book.

"Yes. Whatever" Mr Micah said, "This year we have to be better. Any more questions, new guy?"

"Harrison" Harrison corrected him

"I don't care" he said nonchalantly, "I'll learn your name when you give me a reason to learn your name"

"Yes sir" He said

"Great. Now if we're done with the foolishness, I'd like to get back to AC circuits" he mumbled

"But... Sir" he ventured again and he could see Mariah shaking her head at him out of the corner of his eye. "Shouldn't we have started this prep at the beginning of the term?"

"Shouldn't you have started school at the beginning of the term? Do not make me loose my temper!" Micah yelled. "You think I love teaching dumbasses like you? No. I like smart people, but I'm stuck with an olodo like you, we have to manage."

Harrison swallowed. Hard. He remained silent for the remainder of the period. Micah finally got tired of yelling at a few minutes past five o'clock. Closing time was an hour ago and they were the only ones walking down the path that led to the school gate at this hour.

They greeted the gateman as they walked out into the street. Their school was in a residential area so cars rarely drove past except they were leaving or returning to their homes. The students who missed the bus had to walk all the way to the T-Junction if they were to have any hope of finding a vehicle to take them home.

Mariah's phone buzzed in her pocket as she pulled it out.

We're going out for dinner, hurry home . Her mom had texted.

Are you in the library again? Her mother texted again.

She sighed as she typed, competition prep. I'm on my way.

"Do you guys live close by?" Harrison was asking.

"Heartland Estate" Kami quickly answered. "Not quite far from here. You?"

"Nope. I live at Ikeja. The barracks" he said simply

Ikeja. Mariah pondered. That's really far away, she thought

As if reading her mind he continued, "It's just for a few weeks anyways, till we get a house here" he continued

"When did you move to Lagos?" Kami asked him

"Almost three weeks ago" he said, "My father got transferred, again" he mumbled the last part.

Kami stared at her best friend. She was walking slowly her attention was still on her phone. She was out of it. She hadn't eaten and she wasn't speaking. Granted Mariah wasn't the type to tell fifteen stories in one minute, that was Kami's job in their relationship, but Mariah hadn't spoken since lunch, and that was almost four hours ago.

"Can I have your number?" Harrison spoke up. Kami turned to face her best friend, noticing that she wasn't giving him the time of day, Kami replied, "Yeah sure"

She got his phone and typed her number in. "So your father is in the military?" she asked trying to make conversation

"Yeah. Major"

That explains the military escort. Kami thought. "Is that what you would like to do in future"

He sighed, cocked him head to the side, like he was weighing his options, "Is that what I really want to do?" he asked himself, "I don't know" he shrugged.

"How don't you know what you want to be? We're starting IGCSE in December and WASSCE in April.

"What do you want to study?" he asked her

"Medicine" Kami said, "Both of us"

A car could be heard coming round the bend. Out of instinct they shifted to the end of the road. The car finally came into view, it was a truck. Not a regular truck, an army green truck, the plate numbers were covered and they were soilders practically hanging off the thing. It didn't take a soothsayer to tell that that they came for Harrison.

"My ride is here." he said looking up. The driver of the truck revved the engine sped past him on purpose. Only stopping after he'd reached the School's gate and then swiftly reversing to where they were standing. They could hear the laughter of the other soilders in the van, as the driver honked twice."Yo. Bad guy... Chyke no more. Make we dey go" he yelled. Harrison promptly flipped them off. He slipped his phone into his back pocket and turned back to them.

"You guys need a ride?" Harrison asked.

"We'll just walk" Kami said shaking her head

"Okay then... See you tomorrow" he said as ran and jumped on the truck, holding onto one of the handle bars in the front, he swung himself into the car through what Kami thought was the window. She was seriously reconsidering that thought seeing as she didn't know anything about military vehicles.

"Mariah" she called to her friend.

"What is it Kami?" Mariah asked

Mariah always acted like Kami bothered her. But they both knew that it was the exact opposite, Kami didn't bother her. They both knew that Mariah was alive thanks to Krazy Kami.

"Harrison likes you?" Kami said

Mariah looked up at her friend, silently hoping to read something off her face. Hurt? Anger maybe? But Kami's face was blank.

"That's not true" Mariah said simply

"He was staring at you throughout study hall" came Kami's reply.

Mariah sighed, "He doesn't like me Kami"

"He does. Everyone likes you. I need to know what you do" Kami said

"Act closed off and standoffish that definitely reels them in" Mariah said sarcastically

Kami chuckled, "I should try that. You think I'm too friendly?"

"You're you Kami and you're amazing. Any guy would be stupid not to want you, plus nature always saves the best for last. That and the fact that relationships in high school are over rated anyways." Mariah said. She meant every word, and best of all it made her best friend smile.

Somehow seeing Kami so happy made her feel like Santa Claus."I could talk to Harrison for you"Mariah closed her ears as Kami squealed in delight, practically jumping on her.

Kami the hugger, Mariah chuckled, Like she could be standoffish

Lara and the beat

"Do not tell me you'd give up an opportunity of doing a duet with The William Caiaphas" she could hear her father say as she opened the door of her house.

"Pops, a duet with you is just like white privilege" her elder sister replied

"I am giving you an opportunity that many people beg for and you are throwing it away"

She stepped into the house, threw her keys in to the the heart shaped bowl kept for that purpose and she hopped on one foot as she took off her black converses. She pulled off her black socks as she let her bag drop to the floor and she left them there by door.

"I didn't want to get signed to your label and you signed me anyways." he sister was saying.

She slammed the door with her foot and walked past the large screen door she was sure that her father and sister were behind.

"A lot of children would be happy that their father supports their music career."

"Mariah is that you?" Her mother's voice came from the kitchen.

"Yes Mama" she said dialling her eyes, as she walked into the large kitchen. Her mother was dressed in a black pencil skirt and a sheer white crop top with black pointy toes pumps from YSL. She was rinsing off a couple of wine glasses in the sink. Mariah could hear the clinck clinck sound of her bracelets knocking together as she wiped her hands dry. Trust her mother to be wearing YSL in the kitchen and make it look like she belonged there.

"Where's Christy?" Mariah asked as she turned her attention to the fridge, looking for a drink.

"I have her the night off. We're going... Why are you not dressed?" her mother asked, "Did you walk home again? Why didn't you call?"Mariah turned around to see that her mother was now staring at her.

"Mama" Mariah drawled out instead of answering her numerous questions.

"Let's go find you something to wear" she said, "Pop-pop and Sarah are in the studio, already dressed" she motioned for Mariah to move.

Mariah sighed as she made her way to the staircase and her mother followed closely behind.

"Where are we going anyways?" she whined as her mother followed her to her room

"Uncle Mike's birthday" he mother said simply, "What competition did you go for?"

"I said we were prepping for a competition, not that I went for one. Why didn't I know about this party sooner?" Mariah asked as her mother practically pushed her aside aside and headed for her closet.

"Where's your flare gown"nshe hummed, "The one with floral print, white back ground"

"Dry cleaners" Mariah mumbled, "What are you looking for exactly?"

"We're doing monochrome today"

Mariah groaned at the thought. Her family always had theses colour coordinating outfits that the public absolutely loved. Not that she cared, today she wasn't just feeling up to any social gathering of any sort.

"This one" Her mother finally squealed in delight, "Wait... When was your last wax?" she asked her turning to face her

"Saturday... We went for that thing on... "

"Sunday... right. Okay. Wear this" she said dropping a black leather skirt and a black chiffon button down shirt on her bed. "Wear your heeled lace ups... The open toe ones"

Mariah just stared at the clothes on the bed. "You have to wear a short skirt. Sarah is wearing a striped jumpsuit, one of you has to show your legs"

Mariah groaned in frustration as she grabbed her towel and headed into her ensuite bathroom.

He mother chuckled. "Call me to do your hair when you're done. " she yelled as Mariah angrily took of her clothes and ran the water in the shower.

Her mother was a beauty queen... The best... Won little Miss Akwa Ibom when she was ten, Miss Akwa Ibom when she was eighteen, Won Miss Nigeria at nineteen, placed runner up at Miss World beauty pageant, to Venezuela or some other shit country like that, her mother used to say. Mariah chuckled as she let the water run through her hair that was plaited into two cornrows. She knew her mother remembered the name of the country she lost to she was just annoyed by it. She met her father at nineteen, they got married when she was twenty, which Mariah felt was taking a big risk but it paid off since, they in fact were the perfect love story.

Her father, at the time was the leader of a band that had just started blowing up in Nigeria, Mystic. Her father and his best friends formed the group. Mystic ended up becoming one of the biggest and the most popular bands in Africa at the time. They recorded 4 albums, between '91 and '02 a couple of months before she was born. William went on to hit the peak of his career as a solo artist, writing songs and making music around the world. He started his own record label, Hebstar in 08 and his foundation dedicated to helping uncoming musicians achieve their dreams, in 2010.

Mariah knew what ever path she chose she's still end up in the spotlight, because of who her parents were. Her Mother an ex beauty queen, retired model, 5'11" 160 pound beauty with two children who now ran a modelling agency, fashion/design house and makeup company

She wished she were more like Sarah, her sister. Everyone knew from the beginning that Sarah would be a singer like her father. When Sarah's single had been released and it steadily claimed the charts to number one in less than a week, Mariah hadn't been surprised. She was happy for her sister, she on the other hand... She didn't know what she was going to do with her life.

She laced up her heels as her door creaked open. She could feel her mother's eyes staring at her, practically boring holes in her head.

Mariah stood up from her bed, fully dressed, ignoring her mother's obvious stare. She picked a comb and ran it through her hair, that she'd loosened from her cornrows

Her mother walked up to the table and silently dropped two packets of snickers in front of her. Took the comb from her hand and began to comb her hair in sections.

Mariah eyed the snicker bars carefully, what is she trying to do? She thought.

Myrrh wasn't stupid. She knew her daughter wasn't eating, no matter how hard she tried to hide it. And she knew she'd promised not to force her, the doctor had said so, but Myrrh couldn't help herself. This was her daughter, and she felt guilty.

She watched as Mariah opened up the snickers and bit into it. She chewed slowly. Myrrh couldn't help smiling, snickers had always been her favorite unlike Sarah, Sarah didn't care for chocolate.

Myrrh focused on combing her daughter's hair, she tied it at the top of her head, in a loop. She added the hair extensions and styled it into a top knot. She laid her edges using styling gel. And she finished it off by spraying hair spray to hold her hair down and make it sleek. Myrrh knew a lot about makeup and hair. She used to do makeup and hair for the girls when they modelled in suncity and milan.

"Okay" she said patting Mariah's shoulder and Mariah heaved a sigh of relief."Wear your hoops. Should I make you up?" she asked.

Members of the public had been praising her on how she let her teenage daughter be a kid unlike kids these days who were growing too fast but she knew if Mariah was given the chance she'd cut off her hair and slap a ton of makeup on her face and get multiple piercings in places she didn't even want to imagine. Thankfully Myrrh didn't have to worry about that till Mariah turned 18.

Sometimes she wondered what people's business was anyways.

Myrrh lightly filled her daughter's brows, she smudged a black liner on her eyelids. Mariah had barely any imperfections, Myrrh didn't see the need to but concealer all over her face so she just highlighted her cheekbones and fixed a pair of natural looking false lashes on her eyes. She finished off with a nude gloss with a bit of glitter in it.

"Promise me you'll have fun" she said to Mariah as she sprayed makeup setting spray all over her face.

"I never have fun at these parties" Mariah retorted.

"Try." Myrrh insisted. Noticing her daughter's sour expression, she changed tactics, "Your roots need to be touched up. Wanna go to the salon on Saturday? We could have a spa day and even go see a movie in the evening. What's the name of that one you told me about? Something and the... " she trailed off leaning against the desk as she thought.

Mariah chuckled, "Lara and the beat?"

"Yeah that one. Kami can come too"

"Okay mama"

"Okay" Myrrh smiled. "Let's go down, we've punished them enough"Myrrh commented as they left the room and she closed the door behind them

William and Sarah almost always left them in the dark when they began to talk about music. Myrrh always seemed to focus her attention on Mariah in these times. She understood how being left out could feel. Sarah had a thing with their father. A music thing. Myrrh wanted Mariah to know that they could have their own thing. Regardless of what it might be, modelling, pageants, beauty style, she didn't care.

"Lara on the beat... " Myrrh murmured, "what is it even about?"

"Momma" Mariah said as she laughed. "Momma, I've explained the trailer to you like fifteen times"

Myrrh smiled. Her daughter was laughing. She was really laughing. She wasn't faking it, Myrrh could tell. So what if it's at her own expense... She didn't care. Her daughter was laughing and that's all she cared about.

Myrrh is pronounced Mirh/Merh.Phonetic transcription /M3:r/

High Affinity

"Where's Mariah?" Harrison asked Kami as she walked up the stairs

"Today is Tuesday" Kami replied like it was the most obvious thing in the world. She was running her hands through her braids and tilting her head backward so that they could fall out of her face.

"So?" He asked as her followed her

"Everyone knows that Mariah does not come to school early on Tuesdays and Thursdays" Kami said, "Except you apparently. Why are you looking for her anyways?"

Harrison shrugged, "Is she okay?"

"What?" Kami asked, "Why wouldn't she be fine?"

Harrison shook his head, "Never mind"

Kami pulled him out of the way of the moving traffic

"Did you hear something?" She asked him once they got to the corner, "Did JJ try to talk to you?"

"No. What's going on?" Harrison was confused. He'd been at the school for a day and even he could tell that there was something about this JJ guy that was not right.

"Nothing" Kami said shaking her head, "JJ can be a little... possessive. Especially when it comes to Mariah. So just try to avoid him, okay? Just because of what happened yesterday. Not that you did anything wrong... you know what? I'm going to shut up now. See you in class."

Harrison folded his hands across his chest. His brows furrowed

"Kami" He called after her but she was gone in a flash. Her braids bouncing on her back as she ran up the stairs.

Mariah sat in her therapist's office looking around. The office was familiar, she had been going to this particular therapist for two months now and she kind of liked this one. She usually changed therapists in less than a month, mostly because they always ended up saying or doing something that made her feel uncomfortable. That was one deal she had with her parents. The moment she felt uncomfortable, she switched. There were running out of therapists in the city that she could see. That's why she wanted this one to work so badly. So far it was going well.

The doctor was already in the room when Mariah walked in. She wasn't wearing a white coat. She wore a burgundy t-shirt and a pair of ripped jeans. The sneakers on her feet reminded Mariah of a similar pair she had at home. Mariah loved her style and she made it know every chance she got.

"You like the shoes?" She asked

"Yes. I have a similar one" Mariah replied

"How are you doing Mariah?" She asked. Mariah looked past her and at the wall behind her.

"Has the paint always been this colour?" Mariah asked. There was a table in the room and a swivel chair behind it. There was a book case in the corner, everything was exactly the same. Even the couch she was currently sitting on and the arm chair the doctor was seated. But something was off.

"Yes." The doctor replied, "Why you don't like this colour"

"I do like it... grey. It isn't one of those colour that is shouty and in your face all the time. It kind of on it's own. Not as depressing as black but not and preppy as white."

"A good compromise" the doctor agreed

Mariah nodded, "I'm good by the way. I heard you. I just didn't feel like answering at that time"

"You didn't feel like answering or you didn't know how to answer"

"Both"

"Why's that?"

"Because I don't want to lie to you"

"That's good, Mariah. I appreciate that. So how's Kami?"

"She's good" Mariah said nodding, they usually started out their conversations this way, talking about her mom or her father or her sister, Sarah and somehow, they'd end up winding back to her.

"Kami is good. She is." Mariah chuckled. "You know she likes this new guy Harrison and she is pretty much already planning their relationship in her head"

"How do you feel about that?"

"Me?" Mariah asked, "Nothing. No. If she likes him that's okay."

"Why don't you like him?" She asked

"I don't know because I never said that I didn't like him." Mariah began, "Okay fine. He's just nosy. And because he's new he's automatically pop ular... you know, I don't just get why they like him so much. He's a regular teenage guy"

The doctor nodded, "Didn't you say he was smart?"

"I never said that" Mariah began, "Besides he just got lucky"

"Did he beat you in the exam?" She asked

"No. He had a 96.8"

"You had a 97" the doctor noted

"Yes" Mariah said annoyed

"Why does that bother you so much?" she asked

"Because being smart is my thing. It's the only thing I have."

"I don't think that's the only thing you can do, Mariah. I think you under-estimate yourself"

"Whatever" Mariah said sighing. She didn't like the topic and she wanted it to end. She was sure the doctor could tell.

"How many calories this past week?" she asked changing the subject

"Almost 800" Mariah replied

"Every day?"

"Yes"

"Are you sure?" She asked

"I ate a snicker bar yesterday. Two actually" Mariah added

"Okay. Let's try and get it up to 850 this week okay?"

Mariah nodded unsure of what to say

"How's JJ" The doctor asked

Mariah inhaled slowly, and exhaled. She closed her eyes. Her heart rate was increasing all of a sudden

"Did he hit you this week?" She asked again

Mariah shook her head, "No"

"Then why are you having a panic attack right now?"

Mariah couldn't answer the question. It was like all the air in her lungs was being sucked out. Her vision blurred. She panted. She felt like she was drowning

"Why didn't you break up with him?"

"I don't know... I will" She stuttered

They talked another couple of minutes before she had to hear back to school. Her driver always waited for her in front of the therapist's office while she had her sessions. She arrived school at quarter past ten which was a feat considering she usually got to school at eleven o'clock on day like this.

When she finally made it to class Harrison was staring at her like she'd cheated him out of something. His seat was behind hers, somehow he'd managed to strike a deal that got him to seat there. It worked well for Kami though, she thought. She wanted to be close to him so badly.

"What?" She mouthed to him as she took her seat dropping her bag on the floor beside her desk.

"Miss Mariah," the teacher glared, "Nice of you to join us. Now if you would be kind enough to take your seat, we'll get back to the lesson"

Mariah slowly sat down. "Sorry Ma'am"

Kami smiled at her asking if she was okay. Mariah nodded. Kami turned her attention back to the teacher. The woman was going on and on about something Mariah didn't care about.

Mariah's legs were crosses at her ankles underneath her desk and her skirt had ridden up her thigh a little, she was tapping her pen on her notebook in a sequence.

"Cool beat" She heard a whisper behind her

"Harrison leave me alone" She whispered back, "Listen to your teacher"

"You're not listening why should I?" He asked

"Very funny, Harrison but I'm not you, so listen"

"You two," The teacher called, "Care to share with the class what's much more important than this lesson?" she asked.

"No ma'am" Harrison replied

She narrowed her eyes at them, "Halogens, qualitative properties"

"Melting and boiling points decrease down the group" Mariah said still tapping her pen on her notebook

"Ionization energy decrease down the group" Harrison said

"And so does..."

"Electronegativity"

"Electron affinity"

"Reactivity"

"How many atoms do they have in their outer shell" the teacher asked

"Seven" They said together

"Name the halogens"

"Chlorine" Mariah began

"No let's start from the top" Harrison countered, Mariah nodded

"Fluorine, chlorine, Bromine. Iodine and Astatine" They said together

She nodded and turned back to the board

"Sucker thought she got us" Harrison whispered again. Mariah chuckled

"Bullshit" he added and Mariah laughed. She rarely laughed and she didn't even know whether what Harrison said would be classified as funny but she still laughed. She clamped a hand over her mouth when she realised that she was still in class and Miss Ndi was looking at her like she was about to kill

"Leave. Both of you now!" She yelled

The class gasped. Mariah had never been sent out of a class before. The teachers loved her. She was smart and even if she wasn't listening in that class she stayed silent.

"Meet me in the lab during the short break both of you" She said and Mariah pulled out her wallet out of her bag and walked out of the class with Harrison behind her.

Friends that are friends

"So what are you going to do now?" Harrison asked as they walked along the corridor of the classrooms.Loitering was a sin. Maybe Mariah didn't know that but he did. It was one of the things Mr vice principal had ranted to him about

"I don't know" Mariah shrugged, "I've never been kicked out of class before" She was twisting the wallet in her hand. She was headed to the tuck shop, he knew that judging by the direction she was going in. The shop was close to the class block but not in the same building. It was a gamble heading to the shop at this time, considering that they could et caught but Harrison followed her, his hands in his pockets.

"Snickers" she told the woman at the store when they got there. "Two" she added raising up her index and middle finger. She pulled out a thousand naira noted from her wallet.

The woman silently slid the snickers towards her alongside her change.

"Want one?" She asked Harrison handing him a bar

"Thank you" He said, he turned to the shop lady, "two bottles of sprite please, and Two cakes" He paid for it and they left, walking slowly towards the class block.

"There's an incomplete staircase over there. It's meant to be a fire exit. Let's go there" Mariah said.

The stairs were at the other side of the building. It was closed of because the work had stopped as the PTA had decided that having more than two staircases in a building that housed nearly a thousand students wasn't a necessity. The burglary proofing they'd done at the mouth of the stairs didn't prevent Mariah from going there. The metal bars had just enough space in between them that one could squeeze inside if you moved sideways. It wasn't easy, but it was possible. Mariah squeezed in effortlessly. She'd done this so many times before.Harrison passed the snacks through the spaces it Mariah and then he squeezed in too.

"I think we could be considered friends, we got kicked out of class together" Harrison stated taking a seat beside Mariah on the steps

"I guess" she said tearing open the pack of snickers with her teeth

"Have you tried one of these? " He said opening a bottle of sprite and handing it to her

"What?" She asked taking a sip from the bottleHe held up one of the cakes.

Funtime cakes. She smiled, she hadn't eaten those in forever. "Not in a while" she stated

"They're good"

"I know" she answered, "The pink is my favourite"

The Funtime cakes came in a cylinder about 15 cm long. They were divided into three parts, each part was a different colour. The top was pink, the middle yellow, also known as the regular colour of cake and the last, brown.

Harrison chuckled, cutting the pink off of his own and handing it to her.

"I don't like brown" Mariah says cutting off the brown and giving it to Harrison, "-I gate the colour brown"

Harrison chuckled again. "brown is the colour of chocolate though"

"I don't care" Mariah stated, " Uncle Mike, used to buy this a lot when we were younger. I thought they don't make these anymore"

"They still do. You have siblings?" He asked

"My sister Sarah, she's 19" Mariah replied, "Do you have siblings?"

"Yes, two. Aretha and Manuel. Aretha is two, Manuel is six He's turning seven at the end of the month. He's really smart. Too smart."

"What class is he in?"

"Primary 4. He's going to finish primary school when he's eight"

"That's impressive but let him slow down a bit okay? What's the rush?"

"Aren't you 15 in ss3?"

"Funny" she said, "That's why you should listen to me, I've always been the youngest in every class I've ever been in. It's not always nice. But i think it's cool that your brother is really smart", she added, "My sister didn't even go to a real university"

"Where did she go?"

" Some music college in the US"

"Juilliard? "

"Please, if Sarah went to Juilliard the house would be too small for her head to fit inside "

Harrison laughed, "are you guys not close?" He asked

"We used to be. Shit happened, she became distant, I don't blame her though"

"How's her music career going? "

"Good. She has singles you've probably heard of it"

"Really? sing one"

Mariah hummed a tune. It was slightly familiar, "skip to the chorus" Harrison said

Hold your head up high You're the star of the earth You light up the sky You deserve much more Your heart of gold My lion hearted girl.

They sang the last few lines together.

"That's William Caiaphas' daug.... holy shit!! Your dad is William Caiaphas."

"Yes"

"Holy Shit. You are music royalty"

She shook her head. "Not quite"

"So your Uncle Mike is... Mike Mike? The drummer for mystique?"

Mariah nodded"Okay you get one question" Mariah said, "And I'll answer truthfully"

"Is your sister really gay? "

"Who says that? " Mariah asked

'Every body. That song, Gold? It's about a girl " Harrison stated

"Sarah is not gay"

"Who's the song about?'

"I don't know. I never asked her, I'm just assumed it was for girls all over the world who've been through shit"

"Does she have a boyfriend"

"No" Mariah replied

"Has she ever had a boyfriend?"

"Not that I know of" Mariah said

"Has she ever liked a guy before?" Harrison said placing emphasis on the word guy

"N..No.. i don't know. My sister is not gay" Mariah almost yelled

"Okay o. Whatever you want to believe" Harrison said smiling. He was clearly enjoying teasing her, he changed the subject all the same

"So are you going to do music too?" He asked her

"I don't know. Every one just assumes that I'm going to sing too"

"What is it that you want to do?"

"I don't know"

"So you don't want to do medicine either, like Kami said"

Mariah shook her head, " I don't. That's not my thing it's her thing"

"So why not say that?"

"I can't"

"Why not? Just tell her you're reevaluating your options. If she's your friend she'll understand."Harrison emptied his bottle of sprite, just as the bell signalling the end of the period went.

"Let's go and receive punishment for knowing too much" Harrison said standing up and pulling Mariah up with him. They dusted off their clothes and headed for the chemistry lab.

Miss Ndi was standing in the corner of the lad when they arrived, piling up books, one after the other. The door to her office was in the corner of the lab, Mariah had been there before. It was a tiny cramped space the barely fit the table and three chairs it was made to carry.

"Frankly, I'm surprised at you, Mariah" she said when she noticed that they were in the room, "You're the smartest student here. Why would you disrespect me while I'm teaching?"

"I'm sorry Ma'am" Mariah said at the same time Harrison raised his hand in protest.

"Keep your hand down Harrison" Miss Ndi said, " others might think you're funny but you're just a nuisance"

"Ouch" Harrison whispered

Mariah chuckled. Miss Ndi glared at her. "Better don't let this one bring you down, Mariah" she said pointing to Harrison, "You're smarter than this"

"Sorry Ma'am"

"Wash all the used test tubes and beakers and arrange them properly. You know where every thing goes. I'll be in my office when you're finished"

"We have class in 30 minutes" Harrison stated

" Well then get to it . Punishments aren't meant to be nice"

Mariah sighed as she left the room."At least it's break period now" Harrison said

"Yeah"

"I'm sorry for getting you sent out of class"

"Please, nothing like that has ever happened to me. Getting sent out of class is the most fun I've had in a while. Plus I already know what we were going to cover this week and next week and the week after that."

"Hmm... cocky" Harrison said

"We have geography next. What I wouldn't give to get out of that one" she whined

"I like you Mariah I'm glad we're friends"

"Well sort of friends" Mariah shrugged

"Gaahh.... You like me too" Harrison said smiling

The quiet of broken

Mariah hadn't even stepped into the refectory when she was pulled aside towards the bathrooms.

"JJ" she shrieked

"Shut up" He yelled. He pushed her inside the tiny bathroom stall. "I came to your class during the break, you were out with the new guy. What are you fucking behind my back?"

"I got sent out of class. I was in the chemistry lab. I got punished" she said

Mariah had never felt so unsafe in her life. Panic was setting in.

"So you weren't with that idiot!" He yelled, "Don't lie to me"

"I was..." She began. His palm collided with her face almost immediately. Her eyes stung with tears. She was pressed against the wall.

At least they'd cleaned the bathroom, she thought.

"I said don't fucking lie to me" He yelled. She slid down the wall until she was seated on the floor. She was wheezing and panting. She held her throat as she willed herself to breathe.

"Get the fuck up" He yelled

She couldn't. She couldn't breathe, she couldn't stand. She couldn't even think. Her vision was blurring

"I'm sorry. I'm sorry." He said.

Was he sorry? She thought. Was he really?

"You know how I am. I hate when other guys look at you and that... that Harrison guy. He likes you. I can tell." He continued.

Mariah's breath was finally normalizing.

"He likes Kami" She lied, still holding her throat, "He wanted me to help me talk to Kami for him" She counted her words carefully. Afraid to say anything that would set him off. "I don't know what you saw" She said quietly.

He stared at her as if trying to read whether she was lying or not.

"Oh..." He finally said.

He bought it. She sighed internally.

"I'm sorry" He said again, "Get up, let's go" He said holding out his hand for her.

She rolled her eyes at him. She wiped her eyes and got up. She straightened her skirt.

He kissed her, "I love you, okay" he said.

She looked away.

"I said I love you" He said holding her chin and forcing her to look at him

"I love you too" she said.

"Good. Now let's go" He said holding out his hand again. She took it silently although all she wanted to do was slap his hand away. She took his hand and they walked out of the bathroom.

Kami was waiting with her food when she got there. She took a seat in between Kami and Rebekah. Harrison was opposite her again. This time he didn't smile at her. He didn't say a word to her. His eyes just moved between her and JJ cautiously.

Mariah didn't remember what was served that afternoon, nor did she want to remember. All she could think of was the way Harrison stared at her and how Kami couldn't stop gushing about him.

"You're going to talk to him right" Kami said for the umpteenth time that day

"I will Kami" she said again

"Okay" Kami said, "I just really like him"

"I know" She said

They were on their way to the library. They had study hall till four pm and other students were in their classrooms but she, Kami and Harrison had to prep for STAN with Mr Micah. The thought of Harrison having to face Micah again almost had her laughing. Nobody understood Micah, but he was harmless. Unless words could kill, then everybody in the school would be dead.

Harrison was already in the library when they got there. He had wiped the board down and Micah wasn't there yet, which was unusual. Micah had a policy against late coming. He was never late, if he was late then something was wrong.

"Can we talk?" Harrison asked her

"Sure" She said

Harrison was looking at Kami, "Alone?" He said

"Okay" She said nodding to Kami

She followed him to a corner of the large library.

"We're friends right" He asked her

"Yes" She said slightly confused

"And you wouldn't lie to a me... right" He asked

"Harrison what is it?" She asked impatiently

"Did he hit you?" he asked

"Who?" She played dumb

"I'm not stupid Mariah, JJ hits you and he did it today. I'm surprised nobody notices"

"Nothing happened" she said

"Are you trying to get yourself the believe that?"

"How did you find out?" Mariah asked

He raised his hands up to his lips as if he were praying, "So he does hit you" He sighed, "Oh God. I desperately hoped I was wrong. But I'm never wrong about these things am I?"

"What do you mean?" Mariah asked him

"Nothing." He said shaking her head, "Why are you with him?" he asked

She shrugged. Why was she with him? She couldn't even answer that question no matter how many times she asked herself

Maybe she was sick? Or maybe she believed that she deserved to be hit. Or that she actually believed the sick disgusting things that he said to her.

"My life is none of your business!" She snapped

"Of course. Snap at the one person who sees past this stupid my life is perfect façade that you've put up for yourself. How predictable" he said. He was angry. Maybe even a little bit disappointed

"You've been here two days and you think that you know everything about me. You want to be the hero of this story. But you do not get to save me! This is a fucking tragedy, everybody dies in this one. So do not waltz in thinking that you can change a thing, because you can't."

"Mariah"

"Do not speak to me" She said, "for some reason, Kami actually likes you. So if you want to talk to me about places you can take her to then I'll help you. But if not, don't ever speak to me again"

He stood there silently watching as she walked back into the library.

Micah never showed, they ended up just reading throughout the period.

That evening when the boys came to pick him up after school he had no words and they had fun teasing him about it.

Mariah had a hard time convincing Kami that she had actually spoken to Harrison about her. Because Kami was Kami. When Kami finally believed her, she couldn't stop gushing about it.

The chaos that is family

Harrison made his way into the tiny apartment that had been given to them in the barracks. It had three rooms. It was by far one of the biggest they had here in the barracks, even in it's obvious cramped state. He dropped his bag in the corner as he heard his sister yell.

"It's Harrison. Harrison" she couldn't pronounce Rs so his name sounded more like 'Awison' when she said it.

"Yes baby" He said. She ran as fast as he little feet could carry her and jumped on her brother. He caught her are raised her up, high above his head, making swooshing sounds with his mouth as he held her in the air, moving about so she felt like she was flying

"Higher, higher" she yelled, "Higher"

"Harrison stop throwing your sister" His mother yelled from inside the house

"I'm not" He yelled back as Aretha giggled.

"Stop whatever it is you are doing. I'm not taking anybody to the hospital" She yelled

He sighed, "It's not like I can drop her or anything"

"No, no. no" She yelled when Harrison brought her down and placed her on his side. He walked to the direction that his mother's voice was coming from.

Manuel was seating at the dining table writing in a notebook. Harrison assumed he was doing homework. Manny always did this, acted like he was too grown to care.

Harrison pushed his head on to the table.

"Ow. Harrison." Manny yelled angrily

Sometimes the boy acted like an old man

"Good afternoon, Mummy" Harrison said leaning against the door of the kitchen.

"Come and carry your food, Harrison. I'm not your maid" she said. Her back was still to him.

Aretha tried to climb up to his shoulders several times, he stopped her. When she realised she couldn't get where she wanted, she opted for blowing raspberries at him

Harrison carried the plates to the dinning one after the other. He was keeping Aretha steady on his hip so carrying the plates one after the other was all he could do. He dropped a plate on Manny's notebook and went back for another one.

"You are not funny" He heard Manny yell

Mind of an old man. He thought as he laughed.

"Why do you tease your brother?" His mother ask as he picked up another plate. She came out with two other plates, one for herself and one for Aretha.

"Because it's fun" He said simply

She dropped Aretha's plate in front of him. Her plate was far smaller and more colourful than anyone else's. His mother did it because Aretha was attracted to bright colours.

He placed Aretha on his lap as he sat.

Trusting Aretha to eat by herself was trusting her to pour half the food on the floor and the other half on herself and only succeed in getting two grains of rice into her stomach. As he placed her on his lap she made to climb his shoulder again

"'Retha," He whined, "Just eat first. I'll put you on my shoulder later"

"Tall" she said raising her tiny hands up

"Yes I know. Tall. Later"

"Let's pray" His mother said and they closed their eyes, "Thank you for this food, father bless us as we partake of it, in Jesus name"

"Amen" they chorused

"What are you doing this time?" he asked Manny as he placed Aretha on the table and began feeding her.

He'd been doing this enough to know that if he fed her too much she'd spit out the excess on his face. Just because she thought it was funny. Just like when she had scratched his face and thought that was funny too.

"Quantitative reasoning" Manny said shrugging, "And then I have word problems. It's not like it's hard"

"It doesn't matter what you say, you're not skipping primary 5." His mother said simply

"Mummy, it's not challenging at all. I know everything about primary school already"

"Well take it as a refresher" she said.

Manny groaned. Harrison chuckled

"How's school, Harrison? I hope you're not having problems because we switched you so late?"

"No" Harrison said, "It's going well. I made a few friends then I managed to piss one of them off. All is well"

Manny laughed, "Did you scare them off with your face? Or they realised how dumb you are?"

"I am not dumb. And if you think I'm ugly, you should look at your face. We're brothers after all"

"Oh you wish you could be as fine as me. And I know you had to retake the first school leaving certificate exam"

"Okay. That's just mean." Harrison said, "You know the reason I retook that exam is because I had to have surgery"

"Oh shut up" his mother chided, "Do you really want to be arguing with a seven year old?"

"Yeah... Do you?" Manny repeated

"You shut up too" She said to Manny

"He's not a usual seven year old and you know it." Harrison argued

Harrison noticed that Aretha was fists were balled up.

"What are you holding?" Harrison asked her.

She shook her head still chewing the spoonful Harrison had fed her previously

"Aretha what are you holding?" He asked and again she shook her head smiling

"Aretha if you don't tell me, no tall for you today"

"Hmm" She hummed as her face fell. He felt bad

"So what are you holding?"

She smiled again. She opened her palm.

Carrots.

She had removed all the carrots from her mouth. Then she raised her hand up and all the carrots poured on his shirt.

"Aretha!" He yelled and Aretha giggled as did Manny.

"I need a holiday from this house" She mumbled as their father walked into the dining room. They hadn't even heard him pull up in front of the house. The house was set in a way that you couldn't see the driveway except you were in the living room. And they didn't have a gate, not like in their old house, so he didn't need to honk.

"What did they do this time?" He asked, putting his briefcase down, picking up a spoon and eating out of his wife's plate.

"I'm too tired to explain" She said simply.

"Daddy welcome" They chorused while Aretha was simply chanting, "Daddy! Daddy!"

"Yes baby girl" He said as he got to the end of the table where Harrison sat holding her. He lifted her from Harrison's lap

"Harrison, change up" His mother said, "You should soak that. That's your school shirt and I'm not paying for another one. Manny, bring you father's food from the kitchen"

When Harrison came out hours later, Aretha was asleep and Manny was reading in the room they shared. His father was still in his uniform, only this time he had unbuttoned the shirt and the belt was no longer in place.

"You know what I'll do to you if you ever let your mother do the dishes by herself again..." His father began as Harrison sat beside him on the dining table

Harrison chuckled, "You promise the same thing every time"

"Well, one of these days I might actually do it." He stated laughing, "What's on your mind?" He asked, "Is it school?"

"Kind of. There's this girl Mariah" He began

"Oh, a girl"

"Not like that... she has panic attacks. A lot. She's really struggling, dad. I think she's being abused... I know. I want to help her"

"Let me guess... she doesn't want your help"

"Basically told me to mind my business" he said

"Ah, when people are going through stuff sometimes they don't want to talk about it. Sometimes they are afraid of opening up to someone... of trusting. There's not much you can do if she's not ready to help herself. Just be there for. Show her that you're someone she trust. Someone she can talk to. When she's ready, she'll tell you" he said

Harrison frowned. His father noticed it.

"Opening up about yourself sometimes gets people to open up to you too. Seeing that you trust them, makes them feel like they can trust you" he finished

"Thank you" He said

"Hey, Harrison. I know you were not happy with the move. I wasn't either. But I want you to know that if I could help it I wouldn't have let it happen. I know it's not fair on you guys or your mother to be moving you around like this. But, this school you're attending is the best you could graduate from and it is costing me an arm and a leg, do your best okay?"

"Yes daddy"

"Okay. Go to sleep. You have school in the morning."

"Good night"

"'Night"

That night Harrison sent a text to Mariah

Where do you think I should take Kami to this weekend?

Respect for the Queen

Mariah couldn't help the smile that formed on her face when she saw Harrison speaking to Kami the next day at school.

Kami was finally getting her date and Mariah couldn't be happier for her. She did feel bad about yelling at Harrison previously. The fact that he was asking Kami out kind of trumped whatever ill feelings she had against the guy. Not that they were genuine ill feelings, her defence mechanism whenever she got uncomfortable what too shut people out. That's what she had been doing to Harrison ever since that day.

She could tell that it was taking all of the will in Kami's body to jump up and down in excitement but she masked it pretty well.

"Okay he asked you right?" Mariah asked as Kami strode towards her.

"How did you know?" Kami tried to sound cool but Mariah could tell she was anything but cool on the inside

"I may have left some hints" Mariah shrugged. She did more than leave hints but she wasn't going to tell Kami that.

"Thanks. You're the best" She said, "I hope he's not going out with me just because you told him to" Kami added

"Well, you have to go on the date to find out. Where is he taking you anyways?"

"To see a movie" She said

"How romantic" Mariah chimed sarcastically

Kami nudged her playfully, "We'd probably just grab something to eat afterwards" kami gasped stopping in her tracks

"What" Mariah asked

"What am I going to wear?" Kami whined

"Can you stop that?! I thought something had happened"

Kami chuckled again. "Seriously though, What should I wear?"

"We have till tomorrow..." Mariah began

"Sunday"

"He's taking you out on a Sunday?"

"Yes. He mentioned he has something to do for his mother tomorrow so Sunday" Kami replied

"Okay. So we have till Sunday to find you something decent to wear. We have time. Just call me and we'll figure it out" Mariah finished, "Right now I'm just concerned with whether or not Micah would show up"

"Me too. He's never absent. I wonder what's wrong."

"Nothing I hope. He might have a few screws loose but he's a damn good teacher".

Sure enough Micah didn't show up that day either. The corper took his physics classes for the day. Mariha pitied the poor guy. He's never been in a class full of students who thrived so well academically they made it their point of duty to correct you when you make a mistake. Different teachers had their own different methods of teaching the advanced class. Micah trampled on their self-esteem so much that they said nothing once he entered the class, Ndi asserted too much authority, it felt like war stepping on her toes, Joe the geography guy, told them stories about countries and their differences in relation to Nigeria, Lateef was Lateef. The genius who taught Math and Further Maths. Could shut you up by giving you an equation you were never going to solve in your entire lifetime. Let's not forget Uju, the bio teacher who could slap the taste out of your mouth at any given time of day. This corper had no idea how to handle them.

Miss Ndi took Micah's STAN class during study hall.

Harrison groaned when he saw her walk into the library. "Great. Another teacher who doesn't like me"

"Sit" She said quickly, "We don't have time" She turned to the board and wrote QUIZ and underlined it. "Let's do a practise run on Hydrocarbons. I'm not here to teach you. This is a pop quiz.

Harrison raised his hand

"What?" She snapped

"Is Mr Micah okay?" he asked

Her expression faltered, like she hadn't expected him to ask such a thoughtful question

"Well. Mr Micah is indisposed at the moment. He'll be here next week. Any more questions?" She looked around, "Good. Let's get to it"

"Name the hydrocarbon" She began, uncapping her marker and turning around to write on the board.

Br Br

I I

CH3 – CH2 – CH2 – CH – CH – CH3

Mariah counted, "2, 3 dibromosexane" She said

"Correct"

Harrison stared at her in awe as Kami just wrote down the answer in her notebook.

"Good but you have to be faster" Miss Ndi said

"That was barely ten seconds" Harrison said

"That was twelve seconds" Kami corrected, "And if we don't answer these under ten Pristine would beat us to it"

"Pristine?" Harrison repeated

"The 2nd ranked school in the state. We beat them last year at state" Mariah relied

"And they're stronger this year" Miss Ndi countered shutting them up. She turned back to the board, Harrison heard her marker squeaking but his eyes were still on Mariah.

"2,3, 4, 6 tetrachloro- 3, 8,- dibromodecan-2-ol" he heard her murmur. She was staring intently at the board.

Shit.

"Eight seconds" Kami said out loud

"Better" came Miss Ndi's reply

The rest of the hour spent on the quiz had Harrison feeling more out of place than he usually would. He was smart but damn they were fast. He'd noticed they both had their strong suits. Mariah had all the courses on lock down, but Kami was the bio genius. Harrison could not think of one question they did not know the answer to. He knew he was good at math but Mariah could multiply numbers in her head faster than anyone he's seen before. It intimidated him more than anything.

"How do you do that?" He asked her as they were packing up their bags to leave that evening?"

"The formula is ρgh that's the normal formula..."

"Not that" Harrison countered when he realised she was talking about the last question they'd just worked on. "Naming the compounds. How do you do it so quickly?"

"Look at this" She said gesturing to a compound in her notebook. "There are five carbon atoms but I don't need to count them. My brain sort of just divides them into two. If there's one in the middle it's an odd number. If there's none even. Then I just name it from either side. In the competition they don't give pentane and the likes, it's usually more complex chains of hydrocarbons. Like dodecanols, tridecane, tetradecane, icosne. So you're not going to be able to actually count to twelve, fourteen, fifteen, or twenty" she stated, "It's the same thing with writing down the chain, don't wait for them to finish start writing"

"Have you done this before?" he asked her

"The competition? Yes. Four years" She said

"Four years?" He repeated

"The first time I was in Jss2. I was the only Jss2 student there. We didn't win. I wasn't here though... I was at Surefoot"

"So you were a new student once"

"Yes. And I wowed them with my brain"

"Who was the reigning champ before you came along?" He asked, "Kami?"

"Rebekah"

"Rebekah? How?"

Mariah just shrugged, "I don't know. But she was the best here when I came. Kami was number 2"

"How many hours do you read in a day?" He asked her

"Not as much as you think. Most of this stuff just come naturally to me." she said picking her bag up. Kami had walked out of the library. It was just the two of them now. Very soon the librarian would be telling them to make themselves scarce so she could lock up. Harrison followed her out, his school bag hanging lazily on one shoulder.

"Kami is really excited about your date. I told you to take her to Cherries"

"Sorry. Rich kid of Lagos Island, do you think I can afford Cherries? My father is a public servant" He said

"Sorry" Mariah murmured.

"What? Are you feeling bad for me now? Don't. It's pathetic"

Mariah couldn't tell if he was joking or not. It was bad enough that she'd just assumed that he could afford a place like Cherries. Sometimes she just got wrapped up in her own world that she forgot to check how others felt.

If you are wondering how I know all of this chemistry shit, I am an engineering student. It has been engraved into my brain

♥♥♥

Mae

The cutie

Harrison would have loved to drop out of the STAN if it meant that he didn't have to read and overly prepare. He wasn't one to take stuff too seriously but he didn't want the first memory people had of him to be the one where he quits. He was going to suck it up and read more than he had ever read in his entire life.

He pulled out his phone from his pocket. No missed calls from his mother.

2:30pm.

He was used to waiting like this. Whenever his mother had to have her hair done it always ended up taking the whole day. The difference was that in Owerri there had been a lady who used to come to their home to do her hair.

He sighed as Aretha stopped, forcing him to stop in his tracks. She pulled her tiny fingers away from his. He looked down at her.

"'Retha. What is it? Do you want me to carry you?" He asked in the most tender voice he could muster

She shook her head, "Shoe" She murmured

"What?" he looked down at her feet. Her laces were not undone. He couldn't tell what was wrong.

"Shoe" She repeated pointing at her foot.

"Okay. Okay" He said picking her up. His eyes scanning for a place he could sit and take off her shoe. He found a couple of benches outside a perfumery. He walked up there and sat, placing Aretha on his lap.

"Shoe" She said again

Harrison was starting to think that maybe her laces were done too tightly. He undid the laces and took off the shoe. He took off her socks and she wiggled her toes in delight. Her big toe was red and it looked like it had begun to swell.

"'Retha. I don't know, but I think something bit you" He said.

Most people seeing him would wonder why he was talking to a two year old like she could understand everything he said. He always maintained that children could hear and internalise even if they did not understand. He'd did the same thing when Manny was younger and look what he turned out to be, a smartass.

He wasn't panicking one bit. He just couldn't figure out what could have bitten her and how the thing could have gotten into her shoe

"We're going to need to find a pharmacy, okay?" he said picking her up along with the shoe that she had refused to put her foot in. he didn't blame her, being that he still couldn't find what had bitten her, he wouldn't trust the shoe either.

His eyes darted around trying to find a store that was marked Pharmacy. When he didn't find it, he walked to the list of stores that was pasted on both sides of the wall. He hitched her on his side and she busied herself by stuffing her fingers into his shirt mindlessly humming.

The list told him that there was a Pharmacy two floors down so he made his way to the elevators.

"You see, that button there? It tells us where we are going to. Press 2" He said to her.

"Two" She repeated.

"Yes two. Hold up two for me" He asked and she held up her index and middle finger of her left hand while using her thumb of her right hand to press down her ring finger. "Yes, that's two" he said. "Press two"

She pressed the button with number two. But it didn't light up. "Press it again" She pressed it with her thumb this time and the button finally lit up a red line encircling it.

"You did it. Good girl" He praised. The only other person in the elevator with them chuckled.

"Your sister?" He asked

Harrison nodded. "How old?" The man asked again

"Two" Harrison replied. The man smiled that was the end of their conversation.

When the elevator finally stopped at the floor they wanted to go to Harrison silently nodded at the man in the elevator and stepped out.

"How may I help you?" A lady at the counter of the pharmacy said to him

"Hi." Harrison said placing Aretha on the counter, "Something bit her. I don't know what"

Aretha raised her foot to his face. "It's scratching me" Harrison chuckled as he pushed her foot down.

"Okay. Let me see that" the lady said

Aretha frowned and turned to face Harrison, making to climb onto his shoulder.

"Retha let her see your leg" Harrison pleaded

She frowned, "Nooo" She drawled out.

Harrison chuckled again, "I'm sorry she doesn't really take well to strangers" He said. That wasn't a total lie. The truth was that Aretha followed whoever she wanted to follow. If she wasn't feeling you that day, she could bite your arm off.

Harrison holds her toe so the lady can take a look at it. She pressed a well-manicured finger on Aretha's foot.

"That's an ant bite. Most probably a fire ant" She said walking back to one of the shelves. "Just put this on" she said when she came back with a tube. "I don't think she'd let me touch her" She chuckled

"Thank you" Harrison said as he collected the tube from her. "How much is this?" He asked as he reached into his pocket for his wallet

"Don't worry about it. For my friend Aretha here" She said, "Even if she does not like me"

Harrison uncapped the tube and rubbed the gel on her toe, "Say thank you Aretha" He urged.

She faced him and he cocked his eyebrows. She giggled. She always giggled when he did that, "Say thank you"

"Fank you" She said quietly

"You're welcome dear" The lady said smiling, "Have fun shopping" she said as Harrison hoisted her on his side again and headed for the door.

"What are we going to do about these shoes, Retha?" He asked her.

Of course she said nothing. She was too preoccupied with whatever was on her finger to care.

"Why don't you want to wear these?" He asked

"They pain me" she said simply, "Awison, get another one"

"From where?"

She made a gesture that seemed like she was tired, or hungry, "From the house" She smiled

Right. Because it's very practical to just start heading back to the house right now to get you another shoe. He wanted to say. He sometimes forgot that she was still a baby, "I can't" He said to her

"Harrison" He spun round as he heard his name being called.

"Mariah"

It was a bit weird to see her out of uniform. She was wearing skinny blue jeans and a tank top. Her hair was piled into a bun in her head not like the cornrows she had been wearing when he'd seen her previously. She wore black and white vans and had a small backpack on her shoulder, albeit not the one she usually wore to school. She raised her right leg till it was resting on the ball of her foot

"Yes. What are you doing here?" She asked

"It's the mall Mariah, anyone can be at the mall" He replied

"Oh sorry" she murmured.

"My mother is getting her hair done. I'm with Aretha till she's done" he said

"This is Aretha" She said as smile overtook her features, "Hi Aretha. I'm Mariah"

"Ma-wi-ah" she repeated.

"Yes. Good girl. You're so smart" Mariah cooed, holding out her hands

"She doesn't..." Take well to strangers he was about to say but Aretha totally jumped on Mariah excitedly

"Shh" Mariah said to him, "We're friends now" Mariah cooed kissing Aretha on her cheek.

Aretha giggled and she tugged on the hoops that Mariah wore.

"She likes jewellery. Don't indulge her" Harrison said

"You like this?" Mariah said completely ignoring Harrison, "I have two of them see?" She said turning to show Aretha her other ear, "Want one"

Aretha nodded, "Pretty"

"I know. You're so pretty" Mariah cooed, taking off her earring and placing it in Aretha's hands. Aretha giggled again. Letting the hooped earrings fall from her wrist all the way to her elbow, like an oversized bracelet. "That one is yours. And now we both have one"

"Yay!" She squealed clapping

"Yay!" Mariah repeated.

Harrison couldn't believe it. They were totally conversing and even forgetting that he was standing here.

"Where did your shoe go to, Aretha?" Mariah asked. She was twirling around now with Aretha on her side. Whatever Aretha was doing to this girl was working.

"Awison... memove it"

"Why did Harrison remove it?" Mariah asked. She seemed to understand Aretha's baby talk more than anyone else who wasn't part of their family did.

Harrison would have answered the question but he wanted to hear how Aretha ould answer it and best of all how Mariah would decipher what she was saying.

"Because... Because it pain me. No. no. ant bite me and it pain me and it scwatch me" Aretha explained, "See" she raised up her foot to Mariah's face.

"Oh. I see, it's swollen. I'm sorry..." Mariah began to say

"Did you understand a word she said?" Harrison asked her

"Yes. An ant bit her and it was painful and then it started to itch." Mariah repeated.

Harrison shook his head as if to clear his head. It was obvious he was fascinated by Mariah. At least he thought it was obvious. There were so many sides to her and each one seemed to draw him in even closer than the last. It was like peeling back the layers of an onion. Gradual but he was learning. He tore his eyes from the girl

"I'm supposed to take her to get something to eat. You should come. Seeing as she has taken a liking to you"

"Yeah but don't you think you should get her something to wear first. It's pretty cold in here." Mariah stated

"Awison, say no. He not going to the house to bring my other shoe" Aretha piped up again.

Harrison had no idea she was even listening to their conversation.

"Mariah will get you a new shoe"

"New shoe? Where? Mummy buy new shoe in the house yeteday for me. No. not yeteday. Last year"

Harrison chuckled. It wasn't last year. It as the previous month. But Aretha didn't know that. She only knew yesterday, today, tomorrow, and last year.

"You shouldn't be offering me stuff" He said

"It's for my friend, Aretha here, not you" She said. She was still holding Aretha. Harrison was expecting that her arms would tire out by now, but they didn't.

"Don't you have somewhere to be?" He asked genuinely. He hoped he wasn't holding her up or anything, not that he wanted her gone. But judging by her response he could tell she had taken the question the wrong way.

"Please... You just invited me to eat with you guys. You don't want me gone. Let's go. Besides, I was supposed to spend the day bonding' with my mom but as usual, halfway through she ditched me for work"

"That sucks"

"I know"

Open Wounds

S omehow at the end of that day Mariah found herself in the back of Harrison's mother's car, beside the delectable Aretha who somehow happened to hate the idea of sitting in the car. She was currently wedged between the driver's and passengers' seats her palms on either one. There was no use trying to coax her to take a seat she wasn't going to no matter what anyone said.

Mariah stared at the car seat beside her. Should she force Aretha and strap her onto the thing?She stared at the woman and her son seated in front, Harrison was saying something to him his mother and they chuckled silently. She couldn't make out what they were saying, they were speaking in another language that sounded a lot like pidgin but with a hint of something else. would they care if she forced their daughter and strapped her onto the car seat?

"Mariah I have to pick Manny up, I hope you don't mind..." Harrison's mom trailed off turning into the primary school on the right. Well almost. This was Lagos trust that someone would come from the back and bypass her as if this were a competition.

She slammed her foot on the brakes almost immediately. Cursing out loud as she did.

Harrison chuckled and Mariah seemed stunned. Her mother would never cursed it wasn't ladylike.

When Harrison's mom finally turned into the school she expected her to go out and fetch Manny but none of them made a move to leave the car.

Moments later Manny, or who she suspected to be Manny clambered into the car noisily.

"Jesus primary 5 students are so dumb" were the first words that left his mouth.

"Manny watch your mouth" his mother scolded

Aretha sat on the chair for a second her tiny palms clasping Manny's cheeks.Whatever she whispered to him Mariah didn't see but Manny rolled his eyes and whispered "I know" to her

"Who's this?" Manny breathed out after a couple of seconds

"A friend " Harrison replied

"Well I believe that... She' s way out of your league" Manny commented.

"How do you even know what that means? How do you even know what my league is?"

"Definitely not her" Manny countered

Harrison's mother ignored them. It seemed like she did that a lot. She drove on silently.

"My name is Mariah" Mariah offered

"Ah," He nodded as if Mariah had just revealed a secret that made the whole world make sense, her brows furrowed, "You're the smart girl that intimidates him"

"Shut your dirty mouth Manny!" Harrison screamed from the front seat.

"It's not my fault your deepest darkest secrets come out at midnight and I share a room with you" Manny continued

"Manuel I will slap you into yesterday" Harrison yelled again. This time he was almost climbing over his chair.Mariah chuckled, she had never seen Harrison like this but yet it felt so normal.

"Who would you rant to at night if you do that?"Manny cooed

"Manny, I am never telling you a thing in my life ever again"Harrison continued

"Do you feel like someone with sense now? You're arguing with an eight year old" his mom finally piped upMariah felt herself chuckling. She loved his family. Were they like this all the time? She wondered.

"Why do you keep saying that? He's not a normal eight year old. He's al least 15 just in an eight year old ' s body" Harrison murmured

Of course Manny took Harrison's reply as defeat and turned to Mariah, "Well it's high time you met the intellectual half of the family. I say half but really it's just me"

Mariah laughed again, Manny was really confident and we'll spoken for a guy his age. And Harrison was right he was a fifteen year old in an eight year old ' s body.

The rest of the car ride was filled with bickering between Harrison and Manny, their mother ignoring them and Aretha humming with her fingers in her mouth without a care in the world and they didn't make Mariah feel awkward at all.

Mariah had never been to a military barracks in her life but the movies made them seem like they were always in military gear speaking to themselves in code and blasti ng things into the sky. A little too much but...who could blame her.

The place was a lot quieter that she had expected. There was a clear no honking sign just by the gate. They were armed guards who looked into their car suspiciously before waving them through. They passed a couple of buildings on their side, they were a lot of cars in the lot, maybe some of them were compounded vehicles, Mariah thought.

Apart from the jeeps and limited number of camouflaged vehicles nothing else made Mariah feel uneasy about being on the barracks. She watched the trees pass by as Harrison's mother made a couple of turns and finally ended up on a street that had a block of identical houses on either side. They looked like tiny apartments complexes. She finally pulled up in front of a house that wasn't quite like the rest. I was a small duplex and it had a car port that could only take one car and a car was already parked there.

"Daddy!!" Aretha shrieked when she saw the car

"Is that your father?" Mariah whispered to Manny gesturing to the man standing by the car with his elbow on the hood holding the key of the venza between his thumb and index finger. He was decked in army uniform and he wore black combat boots.

"No. But that's his car" came Manny's reply

"What's going on?" Mariah heard Harrison's mother say as she undid her seat belt and stepped out of the car and so did Harrison and Manny. Mariah lifted a Aretha into her arms and followed suit.

He stood up straighter as he saw her step out of the car , Mariah guessed it was out of habit

"The colonel asked me to deliver this to his home. He said to tell you he was called to the government house on official duty and he will be back as soon as he can" Mariah heard him saying

"I don't understand... he works in the government house" Harrison's mom asked

"No ma'am. The presidency. He was called to the Presidential Villa" the younger soilder replied

Harrison's eyes widened and Mariah watched his mother's reaction. Her forehead creased and her lips were pursed. Like she was trying so hard not to say what was on her mind.Mariah send that meant that something was up. Presidential Villa is a bad thing. Noted

"Thank you for coming" she finally said

"Yes ma'am " he said. He smiled a small smile at them and he walked off.

The house was much smaller that Mariah had imagined. There was a living room that you stepped into from the carport and the stairs were on the right while the dining was on the left. Two doors led out of the dining one to the kitchen and pantry and the other to the room that there dad used as his office. Upstairs had three rooms and two bathrooms and that was it. Not a lot of space.

"Okay. So I'm going to head upstairs for a bit and when I'm back i want you all to be out of those clothes, I'll make some food and I'll drop Mariah off" she said as she made her way up the narrow stairs.

Harrison sighed as he dropped the bags of groceries he was holding on the kitchen counter.

"What's going on?" she asked as she glanced towards the dining room. She had placed Aretha in her high chair and Manny was feeding her banana slices.

Harrison busied himself with setting the things they'd bought in place.

"What?" He asked absent mindedly

"With your dad?" Mariah tried to be as quiet as possible. She didn't want Manny and Aretha to hear whatever Harrison had to say. That and it made her nervous to think that Harrison would not actually want to tell her.

He filled a kettle with water and placed it on the stove to boil. He walked to the freezer and opened it up humming at it's contents.

"Your mum said she was coming to make the food" Mariah muttered.

"Yeah. She's not coming down for another hour or so " Harrison replied. Mariah hadn't thought he'd heard her. "She's praying" he added

"Harrison..." Mariah trailed off not knowing what to say

"Can you make garri ?" He asked her, "If you can come and help me, I need to get the soup ready"Mariah rolled her eyes at his evasive technique but she helped him all the same. He defrosted the soup and he showed her where everything she needed to make the garri was. Soon she was dishing it into plates and Harrison had the soup boiling on the stove.

Mariah washed her hand after she set the plates in front of Aretha.

"I'll feed her" She heard Harrison say from behind her.

"No worries. I'll do it" Mariah replied.

Manny and Harrison refrained from bickering as they ate which Mariah found to be oddly unsettling. They ate silently and soon after Manny muttered something about having homework and headed upstairs. Harrison cleared the table while Mariah red Aretha the same story twice as per her request and she fell asleep before Mariah could finish reading the story then second time around. Harrison carefully pried Aretha out of her arm and headed upstairs while Mariah sat there contemplating whether or not She should leave. The clock in the living room said that the time was a few minutes short of eight pm. She felt the couch dip and she turned to see Harrison had returned.

"You're a good cook or chef. Whichever you prefer" Mariah said nudging him

Harrison chuckled, rubbing his eyes with his thumb and middle finger,"I don't think being able to reheat frozen food can be considered as cooking" he said

"Of course. It takes talent and practice otherwise the soup just comes out bland and the consistency is off" Mariah explained

Harrison chuckled again " thank you for the compliment" he said ," I'm sorry that you had to come here, my mum should have dropped you off first and..."

Mariah held his hand as he trailed off. "Do you want to talk?" She asked sincerely, "I'll listen"

He smiled a little, "Didn't I ask you that and you basically told me to go fuck myself?" He asked

"That was different..."

"No it wasn't" he countered

"I'm serious, Harrison talk to me" she said, she was still holding his hand.

"isn't it late? " Harrison asked deflecting

"I'll call an uber" Mariah replied easily

"They are not allowed here. They have to stop at the gate"

"I'll walk to the gate"

"You don't know the way"

"Harrison!" she scolded

He sighed again. Their fingers were still laced together, "My father gets this random secret meetings. He says he'll be back as soon as he can but sometimes it runs into days, weeks and we don't hear a word. They don't tell us anything. It's exhausting"

"I'm sorry" she said. That was the only thing she felt like She could say. She didn't know it felt. Her father used to disappear for months but he called and his disappearance was voluntary, he had chosen to go. But his was different, Harrison's dad was serving and she didn't know how to reply to that.

"Usually he comes back but waiting is painful. And my mother, I don't know how she does it honestly"

"She prays" Mariah said

"Yes she does" Harrison replied chuckling

"We all find a way to deal somehow" Mariah murmured

"Why are you with him?" Harrison asked. Mariah sighed pullin her had out of his grasp., "I'm not judging you, I just want to know why"

"Maybe I'm weak. Or afraid. I don't know" she said searching her bag for her phone. She opened up the uber app.

"Mariah nobody deserves to be treated the way he treats you" Harrison said

"And how do you know how he treats me?" She looked down at her phone.

Searching for rides close to you

"Mariah look at me and tell me that you think JJ loves you" he said holding her chin. She turned away.

"Leave me alone" she said

"Tell me what you want to say" he asked

"You don't understand " she said, "You won't"

"Try me"

"Your life is good Harrison, perfect even..."

"My father tried to kill me " Harrison said coldly

"Your father?" Mariah asked confused

"My biological father. He's in prison now"

"Oh my God!" She exclaimed

"Poured petrol on me and all" Harrison chuckled, "seems like something out of a movie right? "

"Harrison, I'm so sorry"

"I'm scared of the dark, because that night I actually thought I was going to die. I was six I think" Harrison closed his eyes for a while and said nothing. Mariah just watched him breathe her hands finding his again and lacing her fingers through his, "I think he was hallucinating, i don't remember him ever being sober and i think the drugs made him crazy. He seemed like the kind of guy that would do anything for a quick high"

"Your Mother remarried?" She asked

"She was never married to him. I remember that much, I used to live with her and spend weekends with him. Sometimes he'd forget to buy food and I would starve. I drank beer for the first time because I was thirsty." He exhaled.

"You don't have to tell me, Harrison"

"I wrote the first school leaving certificate exam twice because I was too mentally unstable for the first one to be considered in good standing" he chuckled dryly, " Do you still think I wouldn't understand?"

"I tried to kill myself" Mariah said, "it wasn't a cry for help. I actually wanted to end my life. Kami found me. My parents don't like to talk about it, they sent me to therapy. My father made efforts to conceal it. He said it was embarrassing to his reputation."

"Was it because of JJ?" He asked

"Not entirely." She shook her head leaning against the chair. She didn't want to say more but she opened her mouth and continued to speak." I didn't fall for a guy who was crazy and psychotic, I fell for a guy who was funny and played music and made me laugh and called me beautiful and everyday I wonder what went wrong. What made his change so much, I started to believe that it was mee, that I change him, and then I started to believe that maybe he was always like that and I juts could see it. Or I ignored it. And then I started clinging to the notion that i could change him..."

" You cannot change somebody who doesn't want o be change Mariah. Just like you cannot help someone who doesn't want to be helped and I want to help you Mariah. Please please let me help you." Harrison begged

Mariah stared at him for a minute and then slowly she nodded.

"Do you think he's worth your life?" Harrison asked

Mariah shook her head. "No"

"Good. Because nobody is" Harrison replied, "And you are a strong girl, despite what you or anyone one else might think"

Hi Y'all

I felt like you deserved a slightly longer chapter for putting up with me. I'm finally done with exams so Yay for that. And this story has reached a point where I'm excited about it. We've been building up to the next few chapters, so enjoy.The next chapter is called 'Therapy' and no it is not about her therapy sessions.

Who can guess what it'll be about?

I'll be posting the next chapter by Friday hopefully.

Love y'all loads♥♥♥

Mae

Therapy

I know I said Friday but i was just too excited. Enjoy!!♥♥♥

When Mariah got home a few minutes past 9 pm her mother wasn't happy with her and she didn't bother to hide her displeasure.

"Where were you?" Her mother asked as she walked Into the house. Mariah threw her backpack on an armchair and kicked off her vans silently.

"Mariah I swear to God I will slap the living daylight out of you if you do not open your mouth and answer me right now!" She yelled.

Mariah stared at her. She was wearing a pair of jeans and a tshirt that had a smiley face on it. She was barefoot.

"Harrison's house" she mumured

"Who is this Harrison?" Her mother asked

"A friend from school. We're in the STAN competition together" Mariah replied dragging herself towards the stairs

"Don't walk away when I'm talking to you!"her mother

"What?"Mariah groaned

"What is it? why are you yelling? " her father said finally walking out of his study with Sarah behind him."Mariah your mother was really worried about you. Why don't you calm down and tell her what happened." He asked

Mariah rolled her eyes. "You left me alone there how did you expect me to get home? You didn't even tell the driver to come and pick me up. Why are you asking why I'm late now?"

"Mariah do not talk to your mother like that... what is wrong with you?" Her father scolded

"Nothing. Nothing is wrong with me. So I don't like music like both of you, it doesn't mean that there is something wrong with me"

"Honey there is nothing wrong with not liking music" her mother said at the same time her father said, "I never said that"

"You say it all the time" Mariah said shrugging her mother's hand off her shoulder." 'Oh I'm happy at least one of my children is doing music', or you say, 'Sarah is just like me. She's my real daughter"

"That was a joke, I didn't mean it" her father countered

"I tried to kill myself, and you went to the hospital and paid them money to change my name on the charts because it would hurt your reputation. I was going through a lot and I was feeling like shit and I couldn't talk to any of you. Because you never see me. You just exist in your tiny self obsessed bubble...." she trailed off. She wiped the tears that she didn't know had been falling."When you told me that you were going to see that movie with me I was so excited. It's just a movie but we never do anything together. I thought maybe I could connect with at least one of my parents. We know how that wish turned out..."

"Mariah I am sorry" her mother, " we'll do something next weekend, together"

"Do you even love me? I mean I know you're my parents and you have to provide for me and stuff but do you even love me?" Mariah asked, her mother opened her mouth to reply, "Forget it" Mariah snappedShe said turning around and making her way up the stairs. Mariah didn't stop until stairs got to her room she locked the door and collapsed on her bed in tears.She hadn't cried in a long time, she was mostly numb and just barely existing these days, she forgot how it felt to actually let go and have a good cry.

Harrison would be proud of her if he'd seen her. She smiled at the thought. She pulled out her phone wiping her eyes dry. She saw a text from Harrison.

Home? The message read

Safe and sound. She repliedAre you okay? She added

Yeah. See you in school. Sleep tight came his reply

She smiled. She hoped he would actually sleep and not spend the rest of the night awake, worrying about his father. She couldn't believe she was friends with Harrison. She'd tried to hate him, that hadn't worked, obviously. He was a good guy and despite everything, he cared about people sometimes more than he did for himself. She liked him.Mariah chided herself. Was she really thinking about Harrison in that manner? Kami liked him. They had to be a code she was breaking.

There was a knock on her door breaking her out of her semi inappropriate thoughts. She got uo from her bed to open it and there her sister stood wearing a playsuit Mariah was sure wasn't hers.

"Is that mine? " she asked

"I think so..." Sarah replied, "the temp maid thought it was mine and placed it in my drawer along with my other stuff"

"So you just decided to wear it?"

"It looks good on me don't you think?"

Mariah chuckled, "come in" she said holding the door open wider

"I didn't know you felt like that" Sarah said as she sat on the bed. Mariah sat beside her crossing her legs.

"You don't know a lot of things " Mariah mumured

"Yeah" Sarah said her voice barely above a whisper, "I'm sorry" She said taking Mariah's and in hers, "I'm really sorry. I've been a terrible sister"

"It's okay"

"No it's not. I suspected that something was going on, but I didn't know what to do. You had always been introverted and so even when I saw that you retreating more and more into your shell I just told myself that you were never an extrovert to begin with. I tried to convince myself that that was who you were. But when I saw that ambulance in the driveway, I knew I fucked up. I kept running all these different scenarios in my head... how I could have helped you... I felt so guilty... I couldn't look at you. I was praying that you live and that if you did I would never make the same mistake again. Those three days you were unconcious were the worst three days of our lives. They had to check mummy into the hospital because she refused to sleeep or eat or leave your bedside and she was always crying. Her body gave up and she collapsed on the third day. That was where she was when you woke up. She wasn't at work Mariah, she was at the hospital getting treated. Daddy would never tell you this but he said it to uncle Mark, he asked them to change your name on the charts because he was embarrassed. He was ashamed of himself. He didn't understand how his daughter could be struggling so much and he never saw it. He loves you Mariah and he's so proud of you, he created a whole bookcase for your trophies. He doesn't know how to connect with you because music is all he knows. You know he was never good at school, and you're great at it. You're the smartest person in this house. I wrote that song for you. And I thought that that was the only was for me to let you know how much I love you and how I regret that I didn't do more for you. The song is about you Mariah, you're my lion hearted girl. "

"What?" Mariah said finally finally finding her voice, " so you're not a lesbian then"

"If I woze you eh... lesbian ke?" Sarah threatened cheerily. She laid on the bed and Mariah collapsed beside her. They lay there silently staring at the ceiling.

"You can talk to me" Sarah said turning to face Mariah

"Hmm" Mariah hummed in reply

"I love you sister" she said

"I love you too sister" came Mariah's reply

"Ah... who is this Harrison guy?" Sarah asked

"Who? Who's that?" Mariah feigned ignorance

"Like I'm letting you off that easy. Start talking" Sarah said

"Okay. He's a boy..."

Sarah rolled her eyes, "Obviously"

Round 1

"It was the best date I've ever been on" Kami squealed. "He was so nice and he made me laugh. And after that we went to the arcade and played a lot of games which I totally sucked at in total girl fashion" she continued

Mariah groaned for the umpteenth time. She'd rather gorge her own eyes out than listen to Kami talk about her date with Harrison and act like she wasn't just a little bit jealous. She'd never been on a real date with JJ ever in her life. They never went on those type of cheesy dates that she'd love. JJ never cared. Mariah sighed again.

"And he was so nice. He held the door open for me and..."

"Kami. Hold on a second, I need to talk to Mr Lateef. I'll meet you in there." she said hoping Kami would take the hint and leave her alone. She loved her best friend but sometimes Kami exhausted her.

Kami nodded clearly taking the bait. She walked into the staff room. Did she reply need to see Mr Lateef? Heck no. She just wanted together away from giddy Kami.

She met Harrison heading out just as she was entering the room.

"We must have telepathy or something. I was just about to come call you. Mr Lateef wants to see you"

"I fucking wished for it" Mariah mumbled following Harrison as he turned and walked back into the room.

"Mariah." Lateef said, "I wanted to see you and Harrison. Would you be interested in tutoring the younger students. I'm interested in ss2 and ss1 especially."

"Excuse me sir. Do you mean tutorial classes or one on one tutoring?" Mariah asked

"Tutorial classes. Studies show that students are much more receptive to other students. And it won't take too much of your time. You both can come up with the days that work for you"

"Yes sir" Harrison replied.

When they left the staff room the heat from the halls of the school hit them forcefully.

"So hot" Harrison said

"What do you expect... You just left a fully air conditioned room"

"Well they should 'air-condition' the hallways too" He argued

Mariah rolled her eyes in reply."I heard you and Kami had a swell time yesterday" Mariah commented

"I'm good company, Mariah, the sooner you realize that the better for you" Harrison said

Mariah was forced to roll her eyes again. They were walking up the stairs that led to the floor which the library was on. The first round of STAN was in three hours and they had to leave soon.

"Did you get beaten for getting home late?" Harrison asked.

"Beaten? Who the hell gets beaten anymore these days?" Mariah asked in reply. "No. A lot of yelling, no physical punishments."Harrison nodded sliding his hands into his pockets.

"It was fun. Having you there, I mean. Manny considers you his equal intellectually and my mother thinks you're very humble for someone who's did is a millionaire"

Mariah sucked in air through her teeth, making a tsk sound."Millionaire ke? Is it my money?" she said to no one in particular. "How's you dad?"

"Still no news." Harrison shook his head

Mariah felt her heart drop when she saw the pained expression on his face.She was tempted to touch his hand even if it was just to say 'everything will be okay' but she decided against it balling her fingers up into fists instead she asked, "How are you guys holding up? How's your mum?"

Harrison shrugged, "Aretha doesn't understand a thing... She just wants daddy home. Manny gets it he just tries to ignore it. Acts like he doesn't care, but he does. My mother... I was actually hoping she'd start work so that she has something else to focus on"

"Where does she work?"

"The university. She's a lecturer at... well used to be FUTO. Now UNI-LAG."

"What department?"

"ICT... Telecommunications basically" he said

"Yeesh" Mariah shuddered, "What did she study?"

"Solid state physics"

"I've never heard of that" Mariah commented

"I know."

They walked up to the door leading to the library and Harrison held the door open for here to walk in.

"Micah is here !" Mariah exclaimed. Micah was there his back was turned to them but it was obvious he was the one.

"Good morning sir" They both greeted as they got closer to the corner he and Kami were huddled up in.

"Yes" He said turning to face them, "We're leaving in fifteen minutes get your things. Don't you dare forget anything... we're using the sienna since its just the four of us going maybe a couple of other teachers... I'll meet you downstairs at the Principal's in fifteen minutes.

Harrison raised up his hand

"What is it sir? What? Any stupid questions ... I have returned now go bask in your stupidity..." Micah began his rant of the season.

"Are you okay sir? We were told you were a bit under the weather that's why you weren't in school last week" Harrison asked cutting him off. Mariah stared at him in surprise and so did Micah. He didn't expect anyone to ask or care. He treated them like shit anyways.Micah scratched the back of his head awkwardly."Yes... Uhmmm... My wife died... I needed a few days" Micah said quietly.

Mariah gasped, "I'm sorry sir she said the same time Harrison said, "My condolences, sir... For your loss"

Kami remained silent cooped up in her corner. Staring longingly at Harrison. Mariah rolled her eyes.

"If you don't mind my asking sir, what happened?" Harrison asked again

"She was sick for years... Doesn't really prepare you for the actual death does it?" Micah said. His voice was barely above a whisper. He was letting himself be vulnerable and in front of his students... Ones he ruthlessly insulted and made fun for semester after semester for his own shear pleasure. Mariah wondered how that might have felt for him.

"Okay" Micah said clapping his hands waking everyone up from the trance that they seemed to be in. "Get out of here. And 15 minutes... I'm not joking do not waste my time..."

Mariah chuckled turning to leave the room, she was sure everyone knew he wasn't joking, he was Micah afterall.

Harrison gasped as the sienna drove into the compound that housed the amazing grace e-center. He had never seen anything like it, almost fifty schools under one roof. Mariah smiled nudging his shoulder as Kami took his had poning to the entrance. "This is freaking awesome" he muttered to himself.

"You haven't even gotten to nationals yet" Mariah said chuckling at him.

The hall was even bigger than the compound was if that was even possible. Mariah had been here before so she wasn't staring like he was but he couldn't hide his excitement. He didn't even care if he looked like an idiot grinning ear to ear. Students in different uniforms were huddled up in different areas of the hall. The seats were red and resembled ones you'd see at a cinema. A man stood on the stage with a mic in hand. "Breakfast is served in the banquet hall. The schools that are just arriving should get their tallys and take their seat. Again breakfast is being served in the banquet hall."

"Breakfast?" Harrison queried.

"Yes. Buffet service" Kami replied him

"I'm impressed" Harrison said

"Here are your tags" Micah said handing each of them a thing which they wore around their neck. "Don't get missing... I won't look for you.Go and get something to eat. I'll get the tally" he said walking off. They made their ways to the banquet hall with Kami practically hugging Harrison all the way there. Okay maybe not hugging but Mariah didn't like to witness whatever it was that Kami was trying to do. Did it annoy her? A little Was she jealous? Heck no. She just thought Kami could be a little less obvious. With the staring and the hand hold and the laughing at everything he said, Harrison's head would have to be made of sand for him not to notice that Kami liked him.

After minutes of light hearted conversations over pastries and coffee they went back into the hall to begin the speed round.

The MC was on the stage again and he was explaining the rules of the speed round to the audience. Mariah didn't need to listen. The rules never changed. She couldn't almost recite them by heart. The speed round each contestant had to answer as many questions as possible in the span of five minutes... The key was to pass on the longer questions and answer the ones you were conversant with. Two contestants were allowed per school and you could only switch contestants after you have completed a cycle. A cycle consisted of a five minutes quiz session per school represented, and two minute break. The number of cycles per round is never fixed the end goal is to reduce the number of schools participating to 14. This 1st round is now as the elimination round.

The number on their tally was called and Micah turned to them. "Caiaphas and Abraham." he did pointing to Mariah and Kami. "Harrison you stay here I'll switch you for Kami after the 1st cycle."Micah submitted their names to the governing board and Mariah waited patiently for her name to be called.

"Intense" she heard Harrison whisoher behind her.

"You bet"

Caiaphas, Mariah and Abraham, Kamseobong Their names sound throughout the hall.

"Good luck out there" he called

"thanks" Mariah nodded heading to the stage.

The quiz master rattled out the rules once again and Mariah rolled her eyes again. The virtual raffle draw rolled around on the large screen as she watched other contestants pray that they didn't have to go first. Mariah prayed for the opposite. She wanted to go first. Establish a precedent early. She smiled when she saw the light land on Cedarville. Lighting up the big green letters. She raised her pen up as if flicking her wrist she bit the corner of her bottom lip.

"Five minutes on the clock" he said and the large screen showed a timer.

5:00

"Start!" the clock began ticking, an image popped up beside the clock. Mariah rolled her eyes again

"Name the compound..."

I'm sorry about keeping you guys waiting for so long. Next chapter coming soon. I would try my best to update soonest. Love y'allMAE

Second Date?

They made it to the 2nd round as unsurprising as it was, Mariah still felt a little excited.

The announcement was currently going for lunch but Mariah was far from hungry. She just trotted along with the rest of the students to the large hall that served as the dining room for the day.

Not wanting to argue with Kami she took a seat to her left leaving a couple of seats between Kami and herself for Harrison and maybe Mr. Micah. Who was she kidding Micah wouldn't care about shit like that.

Kami showed Harrison to the chair she kept beside her. Mariah had to remind herself that she didn't care. Why would she?

"Is someone here?" A voice brought her out of her thoughts She looked up to see a boy in a dark blue blazer and a red tie. He was a lot lighter on complexion than Harrison.

"No. You can sit" she said. He pulled the chair out and sat muttering a form of greeting to Harrison who was on his other side.

"My name is Tega" He said holding out his hand. Mariah shook his hand

"Mariah" she said

"Oh I know who you are" He said

"Wow... Stalk much?" she queried

"No. No. Forgive me. I was here last year and you were too. You took it all the way to nationals."

"Yup and lost it there" Mariah said

"Are you kidding? Did you not see what I saw?" He asked. Mariah stared at him quizzically. "The whole hall was in awe of you. How could you not see that?"

Mariah chuckled. "Huh" she hummed.

"Are you always hard on yourself?" he asked Mariah shrugged. He smiled, "So where are you applying to? I assume that you are applying on early admission"

"I haven't thought about it" she said as she watched the line at the service table lessen. "Do you want to go now?" she said pointing to the line

"Sure." he said nodding. Mariah ended up getting peppersoup, a chicken avocado salad and some bread. She notice the salad on Tega's plate, some rice and a bit of chicken.

"That is not food" he says when they got back to their seat and he notices her plate.

"Have you forgotten I have the bread" she said

"Yeah... One slice" he said shaking his head

"So where are you going to do your uni at?" she asked him

"I have a lot of choices"

"Like?"

"OAU, UNILAG"

"You do not have plans to leave the country?"

"There Birmingham and NYU but that's only if I get in."

"I mean you're here so you have got to be smart"

He laughed, "Thank you for that off handed compliment"Something fell on the floor and her shifted his chair backwards to get it. It was then that Mariah noticed that his blazer read Pristine on the breast pocket. She was surprised she hadn't seen the logo before.

"You go to Pristine?"

"Yeah. You remember how you killed me last year?" he asked.

"No actually I don't" Mariah replied, "And no hard feelings. I have nothing against you or your school, I just like to win."

"I know. I feel we could actually be good friends." He nodded, "This is good" he said gesturing to the food.

Mariah nodded. The food was good. Much better than she'd expected. "It doesn't taste like shit like school food tastes"

"You're lucky you get to go home to good food" Tega mused.

"That's right you're a boarder" Mariah noted, "How annoying"

"My father said it teaches you life skills"

"Okay. I don't believe that. I was a boarder at Surefoot and it didn't teach me shit"

"You went to surefoot? I love that school. I really wanted to go there but it was too expensive. Why did you leave?"

"My parents wanted me to be closer to home because they travelled a lot they wanted to be able to call me at any time "

"Can you dance?" Tega askedMariah laughed, "that's so out of the blue"

"I know" he replied, "so can you? "

"I guess so... Though I'm not exceptionally good at it"

"People who talk like that are usually very good musically" he said

"Oh no.. " Mariah replied shaking her head, "My father would disagree"

"He's a music lover?"

"He's a musician"

"Really? Full-time? Has he had any hits?"

"A few. Let me see... pretty woman, My angel,"

"I'm not sure I know it, the pretty woman I know is by Mystique"

Mariah nodded, "Your father is not... Holy shit... Your father is William... That's where I saw you..."

Mariah nodded again.

"I'm surprised you're even schooling in Nigeria sef, OBO like you"

Mariah laughed.She thoroughly enjoyed her conversation with Tega much more than she'd expected.

"Who's that?" Kami asked her when they got in the car.

"Tega" Mariah replied simply

"What did you guys talk about?"

"Stuff"

"Did you tell him you have a boyfriend?"

"Are you the boyfriend police... Kami I'm not in the mood please" Mariah chided turning to face the window.

"Why are you acting like that?" Kami asked, "I'm just trying to help you"

"Kami I don't need your help!... Free me jareh!"

"Why are you yelling at me?" Kami retorted. Mariah ignored her leaning against the window and staring out of it. She wished she had earphones around her to block out the sound of others breathing and the awkwardness in the air.

Kami was dropped off first, her house was the closest to the e-center the competition was held at. Micah dropped next and Harrison shifted closer to her once Michael had gotten off.

"You yelled at her" Harrison stated, "Was it because she talked about JJ?"

"If you're going to probe me the you can move back to where you came from" Mariah retorted

She wasn't feeling like herself at the moment. Theses ghings tended to happen. It might be the side effects of the medications she took ever so often. At times like this she hated being touched, or sitting beside anyone or even hearing the sound of anyone's breathing.

Harrison nudged her, she turned to see a big grin on his face. "You should know it would take more than hurtful words to get me to back off. " He chuckled. The faintest of smiles tugged on her lips. Harrison was persistent, if you met him you'd know. "Have you seen your doctor?" he asked herAssuming he was talking about her therapist she shook her head, "Tomorrow"

"Are you going to take Kami on a second date? She's been going on and on..."

He winced.

"What? What is that face? You didn't enjoy it as much as she did?" Mariah asked but Harrison didn't reply. "What is it?"

"I'm not sure there would be another date.." he began

"Why? " Mariah asked cutting him off

"Well... " he said, "There's this other girl I really really like...

And we have lift off people.I'm excited!!!

As light as air

- -

"Good morning Christy" Mariah said as she got in the kitchen. She didn't like to say that she enjoyed staying in the kitchen more than she did with her family but Christy was the only on who didn't treat her like she was crazy or fragile.

"Mariah... Come help me mash these bananas" Christy asked

"Yes ma'am" Mariah teased walking up to the counter where the bunch of bananas lay. "How many?"

"All of them. How is school? I heard you had a competition" Christy asked

"Yes. And I won." Mariah said smiling as she peeled the bananas.

"So... Where is the trophy?" Christy asked

"Just round 1. We just got past local area"

"So state next?" Christy asked

"No local area has two rounds to narrow the number of schools to three per area." she threw the bananas in a plate and began mashing them up with a fork. "What are you planning on making? Bread? "

"Pancakes"

"Fluffly and as light as air"

"Just like you like it" Christy added, "No school today?"

Mariah shook her head, "What you don't think I deserve a day off"

"On the contrary. I think you deserve plenty days off" Christy said, "Seeing as though you already know everything the syllabus has for you"

Mariah chuckled sliding on the counter bedside Christy. "How is Le boo? Did he apologize?"

"Apolo-wetin?" Christy teased, "Mr Macaulay doesn't apologize."

"Why? Okay did he at least say... Christy you were right?"

"He more like mumbled it" Christy said gesturing with both hands.

Mariah laughed out loud, "He's so proud."

"I know" Christy said rolling her eyes

"But you looove him" Mariah said emphasising the love

"Uh... Don't remind me" Christy said as if it was the most exhausting thing in the world. Mariah knew that she love Macaulay and Macaulay adored her so much. He was just as stubborn as a mule.

"Do when's the next hot date" Mariah asked.

"Do I know?"

"Did you suggest that new Asian place on the pier?"

"Macaulay hates the water"

"Yet he owns a boat."

"I stopped trying to understand certain parts of him to be honest. He threw up right in front of me. On his own boat"

Mariah laughed, "I remember. You told me. Tell him to sell the boat now?"

"For where? That stubborn guy? He will keep it o... Even if it is just to prove to me that he could"

Mariah rolled her eyes. Her face mimicking Christy's own.

"Where's Pops?" Mariah asked.

"Gym" Christy replied, "Sarah is in the studio. Momma is in her room"

"Momma is down here" Myrrh replied cheekily as she made her way into the kitchen where her daughter and private chef were.

"'Morning Momma" Mariah hummed.

"Hey honey" Myrrh said kissing her daughter's forehead, "Hey Christy" she tapped the chef in her back

"Good morning, ma'am" Christy replied

Christy handed placed a stack of pancakes on four separate plates and placed them on the counter one after the other. She headed to the fridge as Mariah drizzled her own stack of pancakes the maple syrup. Her daughter loved her pancakes to be gooey and drenched in syrup so she wasn't quite surprised. No matter how much she tried to hide it Mariah had a sweet tooth and Myrrh knew that.

"Honey do mine too" Myrrh said to her daughter as Christy came back with strawberries, bananas and other fresh fruits. Myrrh pulled the bar stool under the kitchen island and sat down. Her daughter was comfortable on the counter and Myrrh wasn't going to complain about it, she was used to it. "Too much. Too much" Myrrh chided stopping Mariah from emptying the whole bottle of syrup on her pancakes.

"An omelette ma'am?" Christy asked

"Yes and coffee please"

"Me too" Mariah said.

"No coffee mama" Myrrh said, "Give her tea or another beverage like that" myrrh countered. Mariah's drugs had tendencies to make her sleepless and coffee would just add to her restlessness.

"Momma" Mariah pouted

"okay fine... A little coffee" Myrrh conceeded, "Hey hun do you want to come with me to work today? "

"Why? " Mariah asked with her mouth full.

"Because I'm trying to apologize and I think you'd love it."

"What are you doing besides boring administrative work?" Mariah asked her Myrrh could sense that it wasn't a hateful question even if she was yet to forgive her mother.

"We are casting the models for the GTbank Fashion weekend."

"That sounds fun" Mariah noted

"Good. I need a second opinion. Get dressed"

"You're not going to tell me what to wear?" Mariah asked

Myrrh shrugged her shoulders, "Me? No"

Mariah laughed as she finished up her food. They were at the building that housed her mother's company before it was ten am.

"Thank you Amara" Myrrh said to her assistant as she handed her a file containing head shots and profiles kf the models they were viewing today.

"Hey Mariah, " Myrrh gestured to her daughter who was turning round in her swivel chair staring at her phone. A small tendril of hair had escaped from the red scarf she wore on her head. She turned when she heard her name her hoops reflecting the light. "Get up. Who are you talking to? "

Mariah laughed, "Somebody"

"Ooh" Myrrh drawled out, "Later. We'll talk about that later. Right now the models are waiting."

Mariah rolled her eyes and Myrrh thought maybe she was being a little too harsh by one again pushing Mariah's business to the back burner.

"Harrison" Myrrh mused

"Momma!!" Mariah chided

"Ah jackpot." Myrrh continued, "I need to meet this Harrison. If he's making you react like this"

Myrrh continued teasing her daughter throughout the day and Mariah didn't mind it much. She actually enjoyed her day alone with her mother. She chose models who were not like actual models she wasn't into the whole idea of skinny tall models so she chose a variety, she wasn't sure how her mother felt about it but she was proud of herself.

"Do you want to take some pictures?" Myrrh asked her daughter.

"Why?" Maria replied.

"For fun. There's a new kit launching in December. The Christmas editi on..."

" You want to use me? And not professional models? "

Myrrh rolled her eyes mimicking Mariah, "Professional models what do they have that we don't?"

Mariah smiled, "Sure"

"It'll be fun. I promise"

It was.

Mariah didn't notice how much she looked like her mother until they were dressed in identical outfits. And their black Wooly hair was styled into identical braided buns.She really did look like her mum and she loved her mom. Most of the pictures were not properly staged they just danced and laughed while the photographer did his thing. They did a mini video of her mother making her up and vice versa.They ended up getting lunch from Royal Palace and they saw a movie at the Genesis cinema. Overall, it was a great day.

Left Alone

Did she feel okay about inviting Harrison to spend the day at her house? Nope but he was here already. Probably the person at the door. How did he get through security? Mariah asked herself.

"Hi, you must be Harrison, I'm Christy"

"Good afternoon ma'am" Mariah heard him say.

"Please call me Christy. Come in"

"Hi" she said when she finally saw him. He wore a black T-shirt and Blue Jeans with regular converses.

He smiled and held out his hands, Harrison was a hugger, everyone knew that.

She hugged him. She wasn't 5'11 like her mother, she was maybe 5'8 or 5'9 but she didn't come higher than Harrison's shoulder.

"Uugh" she groaned pushing him away playfully, "I was just reminded how tall you are, what are you? A palm tree?"

He laughed, "For a girl you are actually tall"

"For a girl you are actually tall" she repeated teasingly, "I hate when people say that. My mother is 5'11"

"You might want to check with your dad, from what I see he's not a very tall man"

"I'm ignoring you" Mariah stated loudly as she dragged him into the kitchen taking her place on the counter, "if you see Sarah ignore her"

"Considering I don't even know who this Sarah is.... Oh your sister. Why should I ignore her?"

"Because she and my mother have made it their point of duty to... What are you doing?" she said noticing he was staring over the pot that Christy had brewing over the stove.

He picked a teaspoon out of one of the holders and tasted whatever was in the pot. "Mmh" he hummed, "Needs a little... " he trailed off looking round the kitchen

"Christy doesn't like her recipes being messed with" Mariah warned him. She wasn't going to say it more than once because he was just going to do whatever he wanted. Harrison loved food and he knew how to make it well regardless of whatever he might think.

He cut off leaves of what ever bush (technically not actually a bush, Mariah was too lazy to find out what that thing was called) was growing in a jar full of water. He chopped some of the leaves up and added it to the pot stirred tasted and nodded.

"Better... " he trailed off again.

"What are you doing?" Christy asked as she walked into the room with a couple of items in her hand.

"I added cilantro" he said, "It needed something"Christy ignored his pathetic attempt at an explaination. She took the teaspoon from him and tasted it. It surprised Mariah when her face didn't turn up in disgust.

"That is actually really good" Christy commented, "How long have you been cooking?"

Harrison shrugged smiling, "I haven't really been... I just dabble"

Mariah stared at him mouth agape,"I thought you said you could only reheat frozen food?"

"I never said that. I said reheating frozen food didn't count as cooking but I never said I couldn't cook." Harrison winked.

"Okay. You are good but you need to shoo out of my kitchen" Christy said. "I'll call you when the food is ready."

Mariah ended up pulling Harrison away from the kitchen, upstairs to her room. What they were going to do there she had no clue but Christy had driven them from the kitchen and Mariah couldn't think of anywhere else.

"You know for someone whose parents make almost a billion a year combined, I am surprised that your house is this small."He was staring out the window, he took out his phone and took pictures of the landscape surrounding their home. "Can I ask you something?" he asked turning to face her

"Okay?" she asked her eyebrows creasing.

"uhmm" he began, he cleared his throat and walked towards her bed sat on the floor beside the bed, his back resting in the bed.

Mariah was beginning to sense that whatever he wanted to say was important, she sat on the floor beside him. She held his arm, "Harrison... You don't have to say it now... "

"I like you a lot. I really like you" he continued

"Harr..."

"Wait... Uhmmm... I don't know if you like me too you're kind of hard to read like that."

"I do. Harrison, I like you a lot too but it doesn't matter. Kami likes you and I'm with JJ"

He rolled his eyes, "Pfft. I went out with Kami to impress you, because I didn't want you to be mad at me anymore. And frankly I don't care about JJ"

Sure they'd been chatting a lot more recently much more than she even chatted with her own best friend, but it didn't mean that she was ready to be that much of a Judas. There had to be some kind of rule against lusting after you best friend's crush or love interest and Mariah was sure she had broken it. She liked Harrison, so much that she didn't care that her mother and sister were teasing her about it anymore.

"Kami. I can't do that to Kami, she'll be angry and she'll have a right to" Mariah mused

"I'll tell her"

"No you won't. You don't know Kami like I do she's going to take everything the wrong way"

"Well I don't care"

"Harrison... " she drawled out, she was facing him and he was holding her hands. Her brain was working overdrive weighing the pros and cons of this mistake she definitely saw herself making.She saw him inching closer to her, closing the distance between them and she knew he was going to kiss her. She suspected it, she should have moved away but she wanted to be kissed.

When their lips finally came in contact with hers, it was nothing like she'd ever experienced before. He kissed her.

Harrison had kissed her

Mariah couldn't believe it. For once in her life a kiss wasn't forceful and painful. There was no hand holding her throat forcing her head to stay steady, there was no voice in her head telling her to kick the man in the groin that she constantly ignored, bile wasn't rising up to the back of her throat, and he pulled away when she'd wanted him to.The more she thought about it, the more she realised that she'd never felt more deserved and beautiful in her life, and she found herself wanting to feel like that again.

She kissed him. Again. Pressing her lips slowly against his.

Harrison's forehead rested on hers when they broke away. "JJ doesn't deserve you, I swear"

Matters of the heart

H arrison tapped his foot against the wall as he waited for Kami to come out of the staff room. He needed to talk to her and he needed to talk to her when no one was around. If she was going to yell at him then he'd rather she'd do it when no one was watching.

When the door to the staff room finally opened and Kami walked out, h8744e heaved a sigh of relief and walked up to her.

"Hey can we talk?" he asked her as he pulled her towards the computer room. It was usually dark and quiet in there, and rarely anyone except the computer technicians were ever there.

"Sure. I have to distribute these in class, so hurry" she said.

Harrison nodded. "I know you had a nice time at the arcade... "

Kami smiled, inner her was doing back flips and jumping up and down squealing but outer her settled for smiling. Harrison was finally asking her on a second date. Oh how she wished Mariah would skip her doctor's appointment and get to school early. She needed someone to talk about this to.

"I did too... I liked hanging out with you, however if I do take you on a second date that would be unfair to you because, I know you want a boyfriend and I can't be anybody's boyfriend right now"

This doesn't sound like a second date invitation. Kami thought to herself. "What are you trying to say?" she asked him

"I don't want to lead you on and then have you get mad at me for... You know... I just thought I'd let you know"

"Why?"

"Because it is not a nice thing to do. I wouldn't want that done to me..."

"No. Why don't you like me? Do you like someone else? "

Harrison stared, was he that obvious? He doubted it. "Kami, I just moved to Lagos two months ago, I've been to four schools in the past six years. I never stay in one place so no... Having a girl friend is not a part of my plan and no it doesn't have anything to do with me not liking you. You're a good friend Kami. "

"Okay... I'm sorry. I understand"

"Thank you." he said

"Did Mariah tell you that time she'd be coming today?" he asked after a minute of silence. He knew when Mariah was coming in. Between 11:00 am and 12noon. She'd told him but he had to act like he didn't know and ask Kami so that she didn't get suspicious of him or their relationship. If they had a relationship.

Kami shook her head. "Not exactly. When she's done with her session obviously. I have to go" Kami said and headed off in the opposite direction.

Mariah was giddy. She wasn't even expecting to feel this way after all they'd done was kiss but she felt giddy alright and she wasn't complaining.

"Mariah" her doctor called, "Want to tell me how your feeling today?"

"I don't know" she said. Because she didn't actually know. She couldn't explain it.

"Are you happy?" she asked

"A little"

"Excited? Optimistic?"

"Excited. Definitely"

"Why?"

Mariah stalled, how was she going to say this? That one again her happiness was dependent on whether or not a boy treated her right.

"Tell me whats on you mind Mariah" she said practically begging.

Mariah couldn't help but remember the first time she'd walked into her office. She'd found it hard to talk to the doctor even if Mariah had no doubt that the lady had her best interests at heart.

"Mariah" she called out again

"I don't want you to think that my happiness is dependent on boys treating me well" Mariah said

"I would never think that. Plus I think that meeting someone else is the best thing for you right now"

"Why? "

"Well. Normally I wouldn't advise you move from a toxic relationship into another right away but Mariah you have never had anyone else treat you like you deserve. Like a strong beautiful girl that you are. And you need to see how that feels, especially if it gives you the strength to finally tell JJ to kick rocks."

Mariah chuckled. For once the sound of JJ's name didn't make her recoil into her seat in fear and her doctor noticed that too.

"So tell me about this Harrison"

"I didn't say it was Harrison" Mariah countered resisting the urge to smile

"Am I wrong?"

Mariah shook her head this time failing woefully in her attempt to hide her smile. "It is Harrison" Mariah conceeded.

"And?"

"He kissed me. Well we kissed"

"And? Did you feel the intense need to punch him in the face?"

"No. Why would I do that?"

"Well you expressly stated in one of our previous sessions" she said turning over the pages in her notebook, "that if any other guy would kiss you, you would and I quote, 'probably punch them in the face' but you didn't do that to Harrison. Why?"

"I don't know. I meant it,"

"I'm not doubting that you meant what you said. I just want you to understand something. You didn't hit Harrison because he didn't treat you like you thought he would. You believe every guy is like JJ but that's not true. You just have to realise that JJ is a sick human being who needs help. And that is not your fault."

Mariah swallowed saying nothing.

"This is not about you Mariah. It has never been about you. You said it yourself the only thing he has is his music and his parents don't even believe in the fact that he's good at music. He's probably jealous of you, you have two parents who love and support you and your father is the William Caiaphas. He's probably wishing he had your life. You are the smartest person in your school and you could have a future anywhere you want. That jealousy may manifest in the form of aggression towards you and other people, or the urge to control what you do just to make him feel like you're not outshining him when clearly you are. Its primitive but it happens."

Mariah sighed

"You have power Mariah, " She continued, "Yes, you are a victim and he abused you in more ways than one but you have power. I don't think you realize how strong you are. You've been abused and you almost died but somehow you came out of that and went right back into living, laughing, passing, kicking ass at competitions, getting awards... Girl you even modelled for your mom's new collection... The things you do...I' she sighed, "You're a fighter, now fight. Get away from him. Or he just might kill you. Plus I think you and Harrison would make a cute couple"

"Kami might kill me " Mariah sighed.

"Why?"

"She likes Harrison"

"Well does Harrison like her?"Mariah felt herself stupefied by that question. "What are you so worried about?"

"Kami saved my life"

"She's never going to hold that over you head Mariah"

"What if she does?"

"Then she's not your friend. A true friend would never hold that over you, Mariah. Because no matter what you do, you will never be able to equal that."

On A High

"**C**an you believe that?" Kami asked her.

Whatever she was talking about Mariah couldn't quite place her finger on it. It had to do with Harrison, Mariah was sure of that much.She flipped over the pages in her notebook pretending to be interested in the drawing of the heart that lay facing her on her desk. They were having a free period and Mariah would normally read or stare out of the window. Now she really wanted to talk to Harrison and she couldn't.

"Are you even listening to me? Mariah... Biology is not more important than this" Kami whined

"Okay, tell me again" Mariah asked

"Harrison doesn't want a second date" Kami said

"How come you said it in so many words before?"

Kami rolled her eyes. "Okay fine. But I see his point though, four schools six years, it's a lot and you don't even know if he'll be here next term. Technically he's saving you from heartbreak"

"Okay you're right" Kami said, "Yeah student council meeting held today. They're voting for a new Head girl and boy this evening"

"I understand head girl, Anna left to go to university but Emmanuel is still here as head boy"

"Emmanuel just got Suspended"

"What for?"

"His phone had malicious content on it"

"Malicious?"

"Incriminating" Kami tried again

"Kami just spit it out!"

"They found porn on his phone" Kami said all at once

"Oh wow! That's not embarrassing at all" Mariah said. Of course she was being sarcastic, Kami knew that. While phones technically weren't allowed in school the students carried them anyway. And if you were found with you phone it would most likely seized and returned to only your parents. But if you had porn on your phone? That was a whole other ball game that a Mariah didn't know about. And a suspended head boy could never be a head boy after the suspension was over.

"So who are they nominating?"

"You, Harrison, Jeremiah and Isla"

"God forbid" Mariah stated. She had nothing desire to lead the whole school. Not in her life time. "I'm not appearing" Mariah swore, "Try me"

"It's not that bad, Mariah"

"I don't care"

"Look at me for instance, I'm part of the council and I do it"

"Kami I have STAN, I teach tutorial classes for junior students, I now work with my mom on the weekends, I have to attend multiple public functions per week. I do not have the time to be head girl"

"But you have to at least appear before the vetting committee. It is in the constitution"

"You and you blasted constitution" Mariah groaned. School passed by so quickly. Even biology was over before she knew it. It was lunch time and Harrison was gesturing for her to wait for him. She slowed in her steps and he caught up with her.

"I heard I have been nominated for head boy and I need to be vetted? What does that mean? " he asked in a questioning tone

"How's your dad? Any calls yet?" Mariah asked ignoring his question.

Harrison stared at her a while then he shook his head.

"It's been like two weeks already" Mariah noted, "I'm sorry." she quickly added, sending that her previous statement may only make Harrison irritated.

"Yeah. And Friday is Manny's birthday." Harrison said. He was looking down at his black sneakers.

"That's cool. How old is he turning?" she asked

"Eight." Harrison replied,"I think. It's not my business. The boy is too old for birthdays anyways"

Mariah rolled her eyes at him, "so what are you doing?"

"Well we are just going out to eat somewhere expensive."

"Why?"

"The least we can do is act like we're okay right?" Harrison replied. He shrugged, you should come"

"Really?"

"Yeah I'll text you the address... Manny likes you. And so does Aretha. It'll be fun. Friday night. Clear whatever non existent plans you might have"

"Funny..." Mariah drawled out

"So what's this vetting thing?" he asked again.

"Well you get to stand before a committee and they look at your records and decide whether you are fit to lead or not"

"Fit to lead..."he mused "Have you been vetted before?"

"No. I have been nominated once though. I didn't appear. It was just before... You know ..."

"Oh" Harrison nodded in understanding.

Inside the refectory they sat together. It wasn't unusual to see them together, they had been closer since they started practicing for STAN together. JJ was once again sitting on the window staring at Mariah like she had legs growing out of her head.He gave Harrison a once over and Mariah visibly stiffened in her seat. Harrison held her hand.

"He's not going to try anything." Harrison whispered

"Yeah not here" Mariah replied. She knew what JJ could do and she was half expecting him to pull her away and yell at her for sitting so close to another guy.But unlike usual JJ doesn't walk up to her, instead he sends death glares at Harrison, completely quiet.

Kami came in minutes later when the food had already been served. The meal was spaghetti and some kind of sauce that looked like it had gone horribly wrong.

"Is this supposed to be fisherman's soup?" Kami asked staring at her plate

"We don't deserve this nonsense" Rebekah chimed from across the table

"I think fisherman's sauce is as faraway from this crap as possible. This is fish soaked in oil... It's disgusting." Mariah replied

"Is not that bad" Harrison stared earning him death glares from Kami and Rebekah while Mariah just smiled in response

"How you manage to see the good in everything beats the shit out of me" Mariah said

"He's happy go lucky like that" Rebekah noted

"I'm serious. I went to Demonstration College, Warri and Command Secondary School, Owerri, trust me the food here is for kings" Harrison explained

"Demonstration... isn't that they school where they beat that boy to death? " Rebekah asked just at Kami said,"But do you pay half a million as fees at demonstration and command?"

"Okay fair enough." Harrison chuckled Fucking Kami, "And Rebekah, that didn't happen while I was there although I did hear the rumors"

"How long were you at Command?" Mariah asked

"Two terms"

"And demonstration?"

"Two years"

"The spaghetti is somewhat manageable" Mariah said after tasting it.

"See... It's not so bad, is it? " Harrison cooed

"Don't gloat" Mariah said pointing her fork at him. She was acting mad but Harrison could see that she was trying to hide her smile. Harrison liked this new Mariah, the happy smiling... Actually smiling one.

They kept talking till the meal was over and Harrison noticed that Mariah wasn't picking at her food as usual and that made him happy.

They headed for their next class. Amongst the chatter of the 400 or so students the sound of the bell could be heard.

One chime. They still had time. Five minutes precisely.

They had just gotten up to the third floor, when Harrison felt a hand on his back. His hands were in his pockets and he was walking a few steps behind the girls, staring at his sneakers. He spun round and JJ stood there staring viciously at him. Harrison was a probably a good 5 inches taller than the guy but somehow the look on his face managed to make him feel uneasy.

JJ nudged Harrison towards the corner placing his hand on his shoulder forcing Harrison to look down at him.

"What?" Harrison asked. He wasn't scared of the guy, he wasn't scared of anyone who used his strength to prey on weaker people but he could see why Mariah was scared of him though, the guy looked like he could kill.

"I need to talk to you" JJ replied gruffly.

"No need to go so far away. We can talk here. " Harrison replied.

"Great. Leave my girlfriend alone. She doesn't want you... "

"That's not what she said... " Harrison began. JJ had him by the throat pegged to the wall in a flash of a second.

"Say another word and I'll smash your face in"

Harrison raised both hands up smirking, "I don't do violence, man" he said, "Let go of my shirt"

JJ released his fingers and Harrison straightened out his shirt. "Mariah's mine. Stay away" he said and he sauntered away.

It took all of the will in Harrison's body not to roll his eyes at the idiot. "Pig" he muttered.

I apologize for the delay. I got infected with malaria yesterday and I couldn't post this chapter sooner. I am better now (I'mtaking my last dose if medication tommorow) so you'll be seeing more posts from me in the future.

Thank you. MAE

Cuteness Overload

"**G**ood afternoon take a seat" the vice principal said and Mariah did as she was told.

She hated interviews and the panel in front of her just annoyed her. She was determined not to pass this vetting process but her school records were impeccable, she knew she would ace it. That was her fear.

She wanted to skip school today but she'd never skipped school without a reason, and not without her parents calling in advance.

"So Mariah, can you tell us why you want to be head girl?" the principal asked.

Mariah couldn't help herself she rolled her eyes.

"I don't." she replied.

"Then why are you here?" a fairly new teacher asked. Clearly he wasnvt privy of the fact that the school had a system. Why was he even on the panel?

She frowned

"I don't have a choice." she replied easily. She was on her way to tanking this vetting process.

"So Mariah we've taken a look at your records..." new teacher continued, "It says here that you were absent from school on medical grounds for almost two months last year...can you tell us about that? Do you have a medical condition and if so how would that affect the efficiency of your service?"

Mariah stared at the guy for a second. Where is this human from? "Yes. I tried to kill myself and failed so I was put in a psych ward for six weeks. I believe that I do now have the capability to lead others right now. I'm still trying to get my act together. I am in no position to be head girl."

Mariah watched as all of their eyes widened in surprise. Except the principal's, he knew. Her father had told him and she was surprised that he hadn't blabbed about it to the rest of the staff.

"When you say you're not in a position to lead. What do you mean by that?" Mrs Uwana the bio teacher asked.

"I'm not where I want to be mentally, I'm still relatively unstable, I still have to see my therapist weekly. I would be lying if I told you that I thought I was fit for this job"

"You talk about you mental instability here but you... I'm looking at your grades and you don't have a single B, I find it had to reconcile these two things, mental instability and doing well in class. How's that possible?" the male vice principal said

Maybe because you head is like that of a snail you narrow minded man. Mariah wanted to say but she bit her tongue holding back her words.

"With all due respect sir, I was born with my brain. I don't need to read twice my brain runs on turbo speed. I wrote the entrance exam into uni and I scored a 381. I failed two questions on your test on purpose because

I thought you would find it insulting if I score a 100 every time. I'm fifteen years old and I'm in my final year of secondary school where all my mates are seventeen. To be honest, I get bored here, I listen to you talk about hearts and I act like I'm interested when honestly I could draw and label the heart and when I was 8.My brain works fine... But it doesnt help me when it comes to real matters , like making friends, keeping the friends I manage to make... Relating with others, getting my parents to talk to me.. It doesn't help me stop feeling like I'm abnormal or depressed. There's a difference between being mentally unstable and being smart and you can be both. Studies actually show that the smarter one is the more likely for that person to suffer from depression." Mariah concluded.

She almost gave herself a hi-five she was a hundred percent sure she had failed it. No one wants a blabbermouth as head girl.

"Thank you, Mariah. We'll get back to you, just wait outside" the principal said

"And if you could call the next person in that would be wonderful" Mrs Uwana added.

Mariah walked out of the room feeling proud of herself.

Outside, along the corridor were the chair that were lined up for them to sit in. She spotted Harrison in the corner. His right foot was resting on his left knee and his hands were folded across his chest while he leaned against the wall his eyes closed.

"Isla" she called and she pointed to the door. Isla stood and straightened her skirt and walked inside.

She headed towards Harrison"That good?" Harrison murmured when he saw her face.

"Oh yes. I totally made them hate me" she said taking a seat beside Harrison.

"Mariah... Nobody can hate you. That's impossible" he argued lacing their fingers together as. Mariah shifted closer to him

"I told them that I tried to kill myself" she whispered.

"Why would you do that?!" Harrison whisper-yelled. "Do you know that could make them... Oh... " he trailed off his face forming one of amusement instead, "So that's why you told them. So they'd disqualify you."

"Mmhmm" Mariah hummed

"But you know... If I win the vote and you win, we would make a great power couple. You just missed that opportunity"

"Eh whatever" Mariah shrugged, "On to more important matters"

"Yes..." Harrison urged her on stealing a glance at Jeremiah, who was sitting at the far end of the corridor. Mariah always thought the guy was a little weird, he never really talked to anyone and he never seemed to care. In fact those who tried to talk to him said he acted like he was being bothered. Mariah wasn't sure she remembered what his voice sounded like.

"What should I get Manny for his birthday? I have something in mind for Aretha already"

"What for?"

"Isn't his birthday?"

"Yes so?"

"Jesus Harrison... Wouldn't you like me to give you a present on your birthday"

"Yeah but that's because you love me but what do you owe Manny?"

Mariah rolled her eyes and hit him playfully, "Don't be jealous. So where did Manny choose for his birthday?"

"Oh Wonderplace"

"Really? He wants to eat on a boat?"

"I guess so... He gets whatever he wants so... "

"You just reminded me of Kami. Please take her on another date? She has been going on and on about how amazing the first one was... I'm this close to cutting off my ears"

"Aww... Are you jealous?"

"I am not jealous... Okay?" Mariah argued, "I just want her to stop talking"

"Don't worry, I have a great weekend planned for us. We'll have out date on sunday"

"What is it with you and Sunday?"

"I love Sundays" Harrison said in mock hurt

"Where are we going?"

"Someplace you'd like" he replied

"Sunday is my day of sleep." Mariah argued, "Let it be Saturday instead"

"No we're going somewhere else on Saturday"

"Somewhere else that doesn't constitute as a date?" Mariah asked

"No" Harrison replied like it was the most ridiculous thing on the planet, "I would never take you there in a date. What kind of person do you think I am?"

"Whatever... " Mariah rolled her hands waving her hands, "so you planned an entire weekend for the both of us, without my knowledge?"

"Precisely"

"I marvel at you" Mariah teased and Harrison only chuckled in amusement

"Can I have your attention please?" A voice interrupted their conversat ion.The new teacher stood there with a note book on his hand. Mariah looked towards the direction that Jeremiah sat, Isla was a few seats to his left, Mariah hadn't noticed when she'd returned. Both of them were now focused on the teacher in front of them.

"The following students have been cleared for the vote: Baumann, Is-laAkpojevwe, Harrison Okigbo, JeremiahCaiaphas, Mariah. Please pre-pare you speeches to be presented to the school tomorrow. The vote will take place on Friday. Thank you"

"Well, your plan didn't work" Harrison began when the teacher had gone back inside

"Don't gloat" Mariah said pointing her finger at him.

Harrison smiled an amused smile," Look on the bright side. We'll make a great power couple"

Mariah glared at him"I said don't gloat" she warned.

"Let's go, I need food" He said holding her hand and waiting for her to get up.

"Lion" she mumbled

Guess who?

The knock on the door sent Harrison flying upstairs. He knew it was Mariah and it didn't surprise him that she had gone home changed up and was already in his house while he was nowhere near ready.

It was Manny's birthday, it was also three weeks since he'd last seen his father. But they were going to the restaurant on a boat to celebrate Manny's birthday, he didn't want to be sad.

"Harrison.. " his mother yelled from downstairs, "Your friend is here. Tell me if she isn't a human being. She is ready before eight. Would it kill you guys to be on time for once in your lives?! "

She waved her hand gesturing for Mariah to come in. "Please sit." she said, "Let me get these sloths down"

Mariah chuckled and took a seat on the large sofa. "Thank you ma'am. I came with a gift for Manny if that's okay? "

"Of course" His mother said. Turning towards the stairs she yelled, "Manny get down here!"

Mariah winced as she closed her ears with her fingers. Not much yelling was done at her home. She wasn't used to this carefree, barefoot mother figure yelling profanities at her children, but it made her chuckle

"Sorry" Harrison's mom said, "If I don't yell they act like they don't hear me. I don't know what's going on today"

Turning back to the stair case she yelled again, "I am not going to go crazy because of you guys. Your plans have failed."

Harrison came rushing down the stairs.

"Mummy...." he whined.

"What? Tell your brother five minutes. Five minutes and I'm out of here with or without him "she yelled again.

"It's his birthday mummy" Harrison stated

"Is there a rule that states the the celebrant must be present on his birthday? " she queried. Mariah snickered as Harrison's mother left the room.

"Where's Aretha?" Mariah asked Harrison "Upstairs, I think. Retha?" Harrison called, "Guess who's here!"

"Mawiah..." Aretha came running down towards her. Mariah picked her up and hugged her.

"I missed you. I got something for you" Mariah said reaching for her bag. Aretha stood on the couch with her hands on Mariah's shoulder looking for what she had bought.

"Do you know what this is?" Mariah asked.

"Me!" she yelled tapping her chest, "Me"

Mariah dangled the necklace in front of her face playfully and Aretha attempted to catch it. "Can you read that? What is that? What does it say?"

"Me." she yelled again

"You are so smart." Mariah cooed pointing to the letters on the necklace.

"A... R... E... T... H... A" Aretha spelled out as she clapped for herself. "Me!" she squealed in delight again.

"Let me put it on you. Pretty girl." Mariah cooed. Aretha sat on Mariah's lap, in between Mariah and Harrison facing the doorway as she tried to get the necklace on the little girl.

"I'm jealous" Harrison said

"Oh shush you" Mariah chided

"Manny three minutes" His mother yelled again

"Daddy" Aretha murmured giggling.

"Aretha... I told you daddy isn't... " Harrison began but Aretha didn't let him finish.

"Daddy... Daddy... Daddy!!" she chanted

"Retha..." Harrison whined

"Hey baby girl" his father's voice sounded at the door

"Holy shit!" Harrison shouted. His father was actually standing at the door.

His cap was in his hand and his eyes were tired but his lips were curved up in a smile. He winced as he picked Aretha up who had hopped off the sofa headed for the door without Mariah's knowledge. He wasn't wearing his full uniform, he wore a plain army green T-shirt tucked into his camouflage pants and combat boots. "I missed you" he said to Aretha, "Did you miss me?"

Aretha nodded eagerly "Where did you go to?"she asked

"Somewhere really far away" came his reply

"What did you do there?"

"I helped people"

"How? Like mummy? She cannot reach the lightthing. She call Harrison to bring it down"

"Yes like that"

"There is light thing where you go?"

"Yes baby girl" he replied. Mariah loved watching him with his daughter how he painstakingly answered every single one of her questions even though he was tired. Mariah didn't want to say it because it wasn't biologically possible but she thought he and Harrison looked alike, both had this tall imposing statue, they stood at exactly the same height. They had exactly the same look in their eyes when they talked to Aretha. She watched as he fist bumped Harrison patted him on his back and mouthed "mummy" as he pointed to the kitchen.

Harrison nodded and his father headed in the direction of the kitchen, as Aretha kept pelting him with questions.

"What is this light thing?" Mariah asked Harrison

"The lighter. I have corrected her several times already" he replied.

Mariah chuckled, "She's growing. She'll learn in due time.

"How can you not tell me Daddy was home?" Manny yelled as he ran towards the kitchen, "It's my own birthday"

Harrison and Mariah chuckled together as they watched him.

They ended up arriving wonderplace a hour later than they'd expected. They had to wait for Harrison's dad to freshen up and follow them.

Mariah hadn't expected him to be as talkertive as he actually was. She didn't know a lot about soilders but she had expected him to be brooding and silent. But he talked just as much as the boys did and he cursed a lot.Mariah couldn't help smiling at them.

"Harrison" his mother called after he'd put Aretha to sleep in her bed. "Harrison I want to talk to you"

"I can hear you. I'm coming" he whispered as he tiptoed out of her room and shut the door quietly.

"Yes mum?" He said leaning against the wall.

"We should talk about Mariah." she said.

Harrison folded his arms across his chest. "Okay" he murmured

"Is she your girlfriend?"

"No... " Harrison mumbled

"Harrison... "She warned

"Why do you even want to know?" Harrison asked walking away from her

"Excuse me? Pregnancy. AIDS. Sin." she listed

"Mummy..." he whined

"You are seventeen years old!"

"So?" Harrison retorted and she gasped

"Harrison have you slept with this girl already?" his mother yelled.

"What's going on? It's late... Why are you both yelling?" His father's voice sounded. Harrison hadn't even noticed that he was now saying in front of the door to his parents room.

"Harrison is having sex" his mother replied

"Mum!"

He sighed rubbing his eyes, "Come to bed, I'll talk to Harrison"

"No... You're tired... "

He held the door open wordlessly and she nodded and walked inside. His father shut the door and walked up to Harrison with his hands folded.

"So sex?..."

"Daddy please... "

He chuckled playfully. "I don't have a problem with that"

"I'm not having sex" Harrison protested

"Your mother would much rather believe that you are still the innocent 8 year old that she tired so hard to protect, but you're not. And if I don't expect you to have those type of feelings I'd be lying to myself. Just be careful Eh? "

"I am not having sex! Am I talking to myself here?"

"heh... I'm not your mother. She likes to believe that everyone is a saint. But... I'm a realist... You're a human being and you are going to get those feelings it's completely natural. You shouldn't feel abnormal because of that. You know I love God and I try to teach you the best I can about the things of God... However I believe that there's a time where you have to let your children go so they have to choose for themselves the life they want to live. So you should think about this... If you want to abstain... We can talk about that... If not.. We can talk about safe sex too, okay?"

Harrison nodded.

"Good. Bow please go to sleep, I'm on R and R and I'm not waking up till mid-day tomorrow"

Harrison chuckled, "Goodnight dad"

Father, Father

"My father wants to see me" Harrison murmured.

"I don't understand." Mariah said. She had agreed to meet Harrison at Kilimanjaro on Saturday morning as per his request.

"My biological father wants to meet me" Harrison said again.

Mariah swallowed, "Do you want to see him?" she asked him

"I don't know. I should right?" he asked

"You don't have to do anything. Just because he helped create you doesn't mean you owe him anything." Mariah stated

"I don't know what to do" he sighed rubbing his eyes.

"You'll get pepper in your eyes doing that." Mariah said gesturing to the food they were eating. "Are you afraid of what will happen if you do not see him?"

"I know what will happen whether I see him or not. He wants me to live with him"

"How do you know that?" Mariah asked

"He writes me letters. Sometimes"

"Wow"

Harrison nodded as he used his fork to cut his moi moi into cubes.

"Do you want to talk about it?" she asked

Harrison shrugged. He wasn't really sure there was something to talk about. His father who was in prison wanted him to see him and live with him when he got out in parole the following year.

"Harrison... " Mariah called tapping his arm

He looked up, "Are you okay?" she asked him, "Does your mother know?"

"Yes." he nodded, "She doesn't trust him. I don't either. He's an addict. But I just think that maybe I should see him. But I don't know about living with him. I don't think I could do that"

"Don't you get a choice? I mean you're 17 right? You'll be 18 soon"

"I won't be 18 till August"

"Still..." she hesitated, "I don't think he's legally allowed to be your primary care giver... Is that what they call it?"

He shrugged again. "He has no house... "she continued, "No job... No regular source of income. He can't provide for you"

"Technically, he's not my dad" Harrison said.

"That's what I was saying"

"I know... I just... " he put his fork down, "The few memories I have of him are of him pouring gasoline on me or breaking my safe box open to use my money for crack. Not a lot of good ones."

Mariah stirred her drink with her straw.

"My dad adopted me, I changed my name..."

"I didn't know that" Mariah commented

Harrison nodded "He has never made me feel like I wasn't his son"

"Do you feel like you should tell him? Your dad I mean" Mariah asked, "He could go with you there. He is a soilder. That has to count for something right? He can't try anything with your dad there"

Harrison shook his head.

"What is it you're afraid of really?" Mariah asked him

"My dad....he... " Harrison began rubbing his eyes again

"Your biological father?"

"No... My real dad, I don't want him to think that... I don't know how to say it. He's paid my fees, fed me, clothed me.. He didn't have to do any of that, but he did. How do you expect me to tell him that, my father the one who tried to set me on fire... Wants me to live with him. I can't tell him that"

"Harrison... It's not your fault. Okay? Your father is a bum and that is not your fault. But you have to tell your dad. Okay this is confusing...what is your father's name?"

"Prison bae or the military one?" Harrison chuckled

"Prison bae"

"Amobi" he said, "My real dad's name is Oreva. That's my middle name"

"He gave you his name? Sweet"

Harrison shrugged. "Okay let's talk about something else."

"Promise me you'll tell your dad... He'll help you"

"I promise" He mumbled

"Okay." Mariah said shifting forward in her seat as her phone lit up with a text. Mariah's brows furrowed as she read over the text.

"Is that your mum? Do you have to go to work now?" Harrison asked

"No... It's Kami. Someone took a picture of us"

"Let me see" He asked holding out his hand. Mariah put the phone in his hand. It was a picture from minutes ago. He wasn't sure how the picture had gotten to Kami within seconds. They were smiling at each other in the picture, he couldn't even remember what they were talking about then. The angle looked like it was taken from the cashiers desk. Someone that knew them worked here, and had taken the picture. He read the texts below the picture. Kami sounded hurt and angry.

"She says that they are more on the group chat" Harrison commented

"Are you on the group chat? Cause I'm not" she added

"I muted them, sha. Let me see" he said pulling out his phone from his back pocket.

Harrison turned on his data and opened up the group chat. Kami was right they were more pictures there, there was even one the looked like they were kissing from the angle it was taken. They weren't kissing. He was speaking in her ear, the picture made him angry, he was talking about his dad and his problems to his girlfriend, his best friend and someone had taken a picture of that. He felt violated. He stared at the cashiers table.

"Harrison..." Mariah called. He shrugged off her hand and got up heading for the cashier. He didn't think twice about his actions when he saw the tiny boy cower in fear. His raised his eyes to look at Harrison and he stilled for a moment his tongue grazing the corner of his lips lightly.

"Let me see your phone!?" he yelled

Mariah was shocked. Harrison wasn't a yeller... He rarely got angry. But something about that picture got his so worked up. She watched him go through the boys phone and then slide it over to him.

"Why did you take them?" he yelled, "Why?"

Mariah put her hand on his shoulder. "Harrison. Let's go. It's okay"

"What size going on here?" a lady asked. She was wearing the red T-shirt like everyone else. So Mariah assumed she was also an employee. "Excuse me sir, whatever it is you don't have to yell...."

"Do you pay people to take pictures of customers now? Is that what you do here?" he threw the phone in her direction

"James!" she scolded, "I am very sorry sir. I will make sure he deletes them."

Harrison ignored her and turned to the shivering boy. He was afraid, Mariah could tell. She wasn't sure Harrison could tell, "What school do you attend?"

"Cedarville. I'm sorry." He mumbled, "It's just that you saw me and I didn't want to... I get enough shit for being poorer that you guys and not wearing the latest shoes or bags.. It just didn't want you to tell people you saw me working here. I didn't send it to the group chat, I swear. I only sent it to my friend, Okey. He must have posted it there. I'm really sorry"

"I don't even know you!" Harrison protested.

"Harry... Let's go... Please." Mariah sighed. Harrison finally nodded. His rage was pointless now, the deed had already been done and nothing could change it.

"I'm sorry." James called out again as they left. Mariah picked up her bag and they left.She texted her father's publicist. If this was going to be an issue her parents' people needed to be told.

"What are you doing?" He asked

"Texting Nkem, my dad's publicist and my mum"

"What for?"

"It might be an issue. If someone leaks it to instablog9ja, they need to know beforehand.

"I'm sorry I didn't think of how this might affect you"

"It's fine. Its the after shocks of my parents' popularity. I'm used to now"

"How's Kami?"

"Annoyed. Claiming she's going to kill me. She'll calm down eventually. I wonder if you're worth all this trouble"

"Technically, you are dating me and JJ at the same time. I have to deal with your crazy boyfriend, so I should be the one asking that question. Are you scared of what JJ would do?"

"No....Yes... Kinda"

"Call me..." He mumured

"I not going to run to you whenever JJ approaches me"

"You should. He's a bully."

"You are like the best boyfriend ever. And now I really have to go to work" she said when her phone lit up again.

"I'll call you" Harrison said

"I know"

When friends leave

K ami didn't get over it.

She ignored Mariah in the hallways, she never replied her messages, she never answered when Mariah called, she even changed her seats in class.

"She hates me" Mariah stated as she collapsed beside Harrison in the library. He was eating know the library which wasn't allowed but it smelt nice and Mariah was eating better. "What's that?" she piped up

"Chicken jacket" Harrison said taking some on his fork and putting it in her mouth

"Jacket chicken" she corrected chewing slowly. The chicken inside was shredded. She preferred it diced but she didn't mind it. It was tasty.

"Whatever" he said putting another forkful in her mouth.

"Why am I the only one suffering this? Is she talking to you?"

Harrison shook his head as he held out another forkful for her to take.

"How did you sneak this in. Home food isn't allowed in school"

"I just put it in my bag" Harrison replied, "Is it good?"

"Yeah, very"

"I made it"

Mariah sat up in her seat when she heard the sigh at the door, thinking it was Micah, she wasn't ready for his insults. They had won the second and third round of STAN and they were on to the state round. But Micah wasn't easing up at all. But she didn't see Micah, she saw Kami

"Uggh." Kami groaned. She looked like she was contemplating leaving the room. She sighed and dragged her chair all the way to the back of the room.

"Kami" Mariah called to her

Kami rolled her eyes, "I don't want to talk to you" she stated plainly

"I want to talk to you" Mariah said turning to face her.

Kami hissed louder rolling her eyes. The librarian glared at her and Kami glared back. Mariah sighed

"You can go back to being the backstabbing bitch you were" Kami stared rudely

"Kami!" Harrison scolded at the same time Mariah said a hurtful, "Wow"

"Shut up! Okay?" Kami almost yelled. "I don't care what you think. You are the worst human in the world. I can't believe I liked you" she pointed to Harrison.

"Kami would you just listen to me?" Mariah pleaded.

"You are such a bestie. How long had you guys been dating? Deceiving me? I kept telling you about how much I liked him. Did you have fun laughing at me behind my back? 'Oh poor Kami she has a crush on my boyfriend because I'm Mariah I'm so great I have two boyfriends'

"Kami please stop" Mariah pleaded, "I wanted to tell you Kami. But I was afraid you'd not understand"

"Of course I wouldn't understand. Why would I understand how I told I liked him but you went ahead to seduce him. And of course he fell for it because boys are bubble heads when it comes to you. Whether it is because your wastline is smaller than mine or because you are so perfect all the time. Sorry to burst your bubble sir, she's not perfect"

"Kami" Mariah called, "Kami don't"

"Kami, Micah will be here any second. Don't make a scene" Harrison chided

Kami rolled her eyes for the umpteenth time that day. Of course Harrison was taking Mariah's sideHow hadn't she seen it sooner? The stares, the hand holding, the lingering gazes, the smiles... She had brushed it off as them getting closer as friends. She had felt happy, Mariah didn't open up to a lot of people, she could be pretty judgemental when she wanted to be and she could shut people out for days, so she was happy that Mariah was getting a new friend. How stupid she felt when she thought about it.

"She cuts herself. She tried to kill herself last year. I saved her. I did. Me. If I didn't you'd be dead by now.Didi you tell him that? In case he gets carried away by you being miss perfect all the time. Miss 'I'm so rich my parents give me all the money but they don't give me a lot of attention so I started to cut myself and when that didn't work I tried to kill myself' "

"Please Kami could you shout it a little bit louder?" Harrison commented sarcastically.

Kami and Mariah looked up at the same time to see Micah headed towards them. Kami huffed in her seat but she quieted down all the same. Mariah sat quietly in her chair. She wasn't sure what surprised her more that Kami had told Harrison things she'd told her in confidence which such venom that one would think that Kami actually hated her or that Harrison wasn't phased by the things Kami said.

"What is going on here? What's the matter?" Micah asked looking between the them. Both girls looked away avoiding his prying eyes, Kami stared at the bookcase beside her and Mariah looked down at her notebook.

Harrison cleared his throat, "Uhm..."He began but he was cut off by Micah saying, "I do not care. Keep you little children problems to yourself. Just don't let it affect my competition, okay?"

"Yes sir" they murmured at once.

"Good. Now let's talk about magnetism"

Mariah sighed again, pulling her notebook out of her bag. She felt Harrison squeeze her hand under the desk and the corners of her lips curved up in a smile.

Micah's lecture took the usual hour and a half with an extra half hour of raining abuses on them, making sure to remind them of their incompete ncies.She excused herself to go to the bathroom and right after that Micah packed up his things and made his way out of the library.

Harrison got up picking up Mariah's bag and his own. Waving to signify to the librarian that they were going to leave in a second. "Kami... "

"Please don't... I'm not about to listen to any pitiful excuse you have to tell me" Kami seethed

"Good because I'm not going to give you any excuses. I like Mariah. I love her and I don't need permission from you to date her."

"You lied to me"

"We went on one date, Kami. I doubt that qualifies as cheating on you. You are quick to blab your mouth when something bad happens, it makes you a terrible friend"

"She told you"

"Yes. And you know why she tried to kill herself? JJ was abusing her... Still is but you are so wrapped up in getting everything to be about you that you can't even see that she's struggling. Heck I've been here two fucking months and I can already tell. She didn't try to kill herself because she was seeking attention it's because she was tired of being alone... Because even with you around she still felt like she was drowning. So o think, Kami that you are the reason she tried to kill herself, I mean if she couldn't talk to you then who was she going to be able to talk to? So before you pride yourself as being the best best friend ever, why don't you reevaluate yourself. Because if didn't notice what she was going through then that goes to show how selfish and self centered you are and if you noticed and you decided to ignore it then you are a terrible human being"

Power

- -

Mariah was dragged into the bathroom for the umpteenth time in her short number of years on this earth. This time she wasn't afraid, she was annoyed. She had the state round of STAN in two hours and JJ was trying to exert his pathetic sense of masculinity again. Micah was probably waiting for her in the parking lot.

"What is it JJ?" she asked

"Is is me you're talking to like that?" he asked

"No... your ancestors" she replied sarcastically

The sound of his palm hitting her card echoed throughout the tiny stall. "You really are crazy! Is it because of that small boy? You're talking back? To me? Me? JJ... Your own boyfriend?"

The anger in his voice almost made her cower back in fear. His hair was spiky, he always had it done that day? Had she liked his hair that way? Ever? Because he looked insane, she barely stiffled a laugh. What did she really like about him? She couldn't place her finger on it. Maybe she liked him because he sang really well... She almost laughed at herself and her stupid sense of reasoning.

"Something funny?" he asked her

"Mmhmm" she hummed

"Tell me before I bust your head open" he seethed

"You." she said and he slapped her again. Her tongue got caught in between her teeth and she tasted blood in her mouth. She spat into the sink behind her.

"I think that guy that you're cheating on me with is getting ideas into you head. What did he tell you? That you're beautiful? That you deserve the world? Oh that he's in love with you?"

"Yes" she replied. JJ slapped her again.

"Ashawo... Na so you dey give everybody abi?" he yelled.

"Yes." she replied again. Something about being able to talk back to him made her feel powerful. Strong.

"You are a prostitute!!"

His voice was getting louder, Mariah knew with time he would attract people onto their floor. She was starting to worry that it was taking too long.

"I love you" he stated. Mariah ignored him. She wasn't going to dignify that statement with a reply. "I said I love you!" he said again, this time a lot louder.

"Tell me you love me. Say it!" he yelled again

"You wish somebody loved you JJ" she seethed

His hand rose from her wrist and slowly rested against her throat. Then he added pressure slowly, she spluttered and choked and he smiled his lips curling up to the side.

"Not mouthing off right now are you?" he teased increasing the pressure on her neck. The insane look in his eyes, she felt like she was really doing to die

She spluttered up words that were indecipherable. "What are you saying? Begging me to let you live are you?" he yelled again.

Mariah tried talking again but nothing was coming out. He released his had just a bit and she was able to take air into her lungs.

"Fuck you" she yelled.

"Ha you can talk now?" JJ yelled, "Let's see how much longer you can stay, Ashawo from the gutter"

Mariah forced her face to twist up in a smile. If JJ was going to play mind games. She was going to do it to. She smiled.

"I slept with him" she whispered smiling, "I did"

Mariah could have sworn she saw JJ's eyes go ten times darker. It was like something was possessing him.

"You're lying. You're a liar" He yelled

"But I did" Mariah whispered again.

"You told me you were a virgin. You said you were not ready. "

"I lied" Mariah said

JJ groaned loudly smashing her head against the door of the bathroom. Mariah fell limp against the floor. She felt thick warm liquid dripping down the side of her face. She touched it with her hand.

Blood.

She closed her right eye. Feeling for the wound, her head was throbbing badly.

"Fuck! Why did you have to say that. Why? Why? Why? I don't want to kill you. Why did you have to go and make me angry like that" he was pacing and his fists were slamming into anything that he could find.

She tried to stand. She wobbled on her feet. Her vision was getting blurry and her eyes were heavy. She wanted to hold out till she heard footsteps or someone wanted to use the bathroom. She had seen the stages of JJ's rage multiple times. Right now if she didn't apologize, he was going to get even angrier, but she wasn't going to apologize. She wanted him to get angry. She leaned against the wall, taking in deep breaths.

"You will go out there and you will tell him that do not love him anymore and you want to stay with me." he said.

Mariah chuckled, "No" she said as she shook her head.

"Mariah... Don't get me angry. You love me"

"I love Harrison"

"You love me, right? " he asked even louder. His hand pressing against her neck again. Mariah took a deep breath.

"Not even a single bit" she mused and he slammed her against the door of the stall again. This time her whole body shook with pain.

"You cannot leave me Mariah. I love you. Say you love me too!" he yelled as he pressed her against the door applying pressure to her neck. He lifted her up and her feet were dangling in the air, he slammed her to the ground again. "You love me. You love me!" he cried delivering punch after punch to her scrunched up frame on the floor.

"You love me! You have to love me!"

Voices were heard just outside the door. It sounded like they were yelling. Mariah couldn't hear properly and JJ was too busy being angry to care. Mariah felt her body giving away slowly. She was hurting all over but she kept chiding herself to stay awake. She heard the banging on the door. Someone was forcing their way in.

She wasn't going to die after all.

Deja-Vu

The sound of beeping heart rate monitors only served to annoy Mariah. It wasn't her first time in a hospital bed, the first time around she felt like a failure that she had failed at one more thing in her life and the heart rate monitors served to remind her that she had failed at such a simple task as killing herself. But this time she wanted to wake up and the monitors only bothered her because they were loud and her head throbbed. She felt like she had been hit by a car and she did not even remember why she felt like that.

She raised her head up. Well she tried to. It throbbed, badly. She groaned staring at the ceiling defeatedly. Eyes hovered above her.

Six pairs of eyes. No three. She counted as her gaze steadied.

There was a loud beep in the room and voices sounded over the speaker paging a doctor somewhere.

"Too loud" she grumbled.

"Oh my God she's awake" someone said.

"Mariah, Mariah how are you feeling?" some one else asked.

"I'll call the doctor" the third person said leaving the room.

She groaned again.

"Do you think she's okay?" one said to the other, "The doctor said she might it remember a lot"

She winced and closed her eyes again.

"Good morning," the man in the white coat said, "Can you hear me?" he said standing beside her head and snapping his fingers around her ears"

She nodded, "Loudly" her voice came out as a hoarse whisper.

"Can you tell me your name?" He asked, "Your full name" He added quickly.

"Mariah Asari Caiaphas"

"How old are you?"

"15"

"What is today's date?"

Mariah rolled her eyes, "I don't know I just woke up. The last thing I remember is that I had STAN... shit, STAN... Micah is going to kill me"

"Relax, hun we took care of that... "

"Took care of what? I need to be at that competition"

"That competition was yesterday"

"What? Why am I here...? "

"What do you remember about yesterday, Mariah?"

"I was supposed to have STAN and... " she trailed off... "Where is Harrison?"

"He's at school Mariah" one of the other people in the room said.

"Can you name the people in this room?" the doctor asked.

Mariah groaned and rolled her eyes. It was like the first time she woke up in a hospital the first time all over again. Of course she remembered who they were

"Momma, Pop-Pop, Sister" she recited and she could swear she heard them sigh in relief. Her sister was leaning against the wall avoiding her gaze. Her parents were beside the doctor, he mother was fiddling with her inch long acrylic nails and her dad's arms were folded across his chest. His sleeves were rolled up. Occassionally he would look over at his wife and squeeze her shoulder in assurance? Support? Mariah didn't know

"Good now can you tell me their names?"

Mariah winced. She felt pain above her right eyebrow.

"Williams, Myrrh... What's the other one's name?" Mariah said in a poor attempt of a joke.

Sarah gasped and her parents eyes widened in confusion.

"Relax... I was kidding, Sarah. How could I forget"

"Do you remember how you ended up in the hospital?"

Mariah nodded, "Cab you tell me what you remember?" the doctor asked

"I'd rather not, thank you very miuch" she replied

"Mariah just do what the doctor says" her father attempted to scold her but it just came out as a scared whisper.

"JJ... He pulled me into the bathroom... I was on my was to the car park" Mariah closed her eyes, "He was angry, really angry and he hit me a lot... I was bleeding and someone was banging on the door. I don't remember anything other than that?"

"Who is this JJ guy...? Is he one of your friends?" her sister asked

Mariah scoffed, "No. He's someone I used to date"

"You used to date someone?" Her father yelled "You used to date someone?" his voice was getting louder every second.

Mariah held her head, "Oh Christ"

"I don't advice you yelling him the room sir," The young doctor began.

"Get out" Her father seethed pointing at the door

He doctor hurries out and Mariah rolled her eyes again

"William...hun.." He mother tried but her father was long gone Mariah knew it.

"You were dating someone? At 15? And a psychopath at that?"

"Pops... She's obviously not well and your voice is really loud" Sarah tried calming him down.

"Did you know about this?" He asked turning to Sarah

Sarah moved away from the wall and walked towards the bed, "No. But I know about Harrison and besides I don't see anything wrong with her dating"

"Honey... You should have told me, maybe if we'd me this JJ guy we would have known if he was good for you or not"

"You are encouraging her... Why are you encouraging her? She's 15 years old!" he shrieked, "And who's this Harrison again. Another guy? What is wrong with you Mariah? Why are you hell bent on giving me a heart attack. I didn't have this much problems with your sister when she was your age"

"Oh shut up William" Myrrh yelled like she had had enough. "She's not Sarah... Stop comparing her to Sarah. You have two daughters William, learn to love them both"

Sarah shot her an apologetic look and Mariah shrugged it off.

"If you guys are done making this about you... I'm hungry" Mariah said

"Oh hun, Christy is coming with food. She'll be here in a few minutes. And Harrison was here yesterday, he said he'll drop by after school today. And tomorrow is Saturday so he might be here too. Kami came around... Although she didn't want to come in and sit with you, did you guys have a fight?"

Mariah ignored her mother's question and asked her own, "It wasn't Harrison who found me?"

"No." Her mother said, "So you and Kami fought. You're avoiding my question. What happened? You guys have been friends for a while"

"Who found me then?" Mariah asked. She was silently hoping that it wasn't Kami because she couldn't owe the girl twice her life. Especially when she rubbed it in her face like she did recently.

"Your teacher, Micah"

Haha.... Gotcha Y'all thought it was Harrison right? Naaah... We're going to see a new side of Micah soon so brace yourselves.

MAE

Lyrical Genius

Christy brought over over fried rice which she made. It was garnished with a lot of good stuff and Mariah ate more than she had in a while. Christy had cleared out the plates and was washed them off in the bathroom that adjoined her private room.

Her father walked in the room as she was sipping her drink from the twirly straw that made her feel like she was an absolute child.

"Mariah." He called pulling a chair to sit beside her bed.

"Father" She said

"Haha" He chuckled dryly

"Yes daddy?" Her said with fake enthusiasm

"I love you" he said

"What?"

"I don't want you to ever think that I don't love you or I don't care about you. Or that I wish that you were someone else"

"But you wish I was more like Sarah" Mariah stated finally dropping her cup with the twirly straw on the bedside table.

"No. No. " he said shaking his head. "You go through so much. I just wish I could take away some of the pain for you. And sometimes i just wonder if maybe it would be easier for you if you were more like Sarah."

"Aww... Pops" she said, "You almost sound like you're trying out new lyrics on me"

He chuckled. "I wouldn't never do that bear. It's awful not to mention corny"

"Ah" Mariah nodded in understanding

"Did I use the word corny correctly?" He asked

"Yes Pops"

"Okay good. You are smart so smart and you want to be a doctor... I don't even know... "He trailed off running his hands through his hair. He rolled his chair even closer to the bed and placed his elbows on the mattress. "I wasn't exactly the brightest in school" he said

"I know Pops" She said almost chuckling

"No I'm serious... I was one of those guys that used to sit at the back and draw in their notebooks. Except mine wasn't drawing, it was lyrics. Songs. And this wasn't a case of me not even applying myself... I was just dumb when it came to school work. I used to feel so lost but when it came to music... Any kind of music, I understood it perfectly. I used to be one of those kids to make fun of the smarter ones... Because we couldn't be like them we sat at the back of the class and coined ridiculous nicknames for them. When my daughter grew up to be even smarter that the guys I used to bully in school... I just thought how much harder your life was going to be. That's why I made you leave Surefoot ...to this school for the gifted you now currently attend. Being smart is okay there and I like that"

"I'm not that smart." Mariah shrugged, "I couldn't figure out that JJ was eventually going to kill me"

"Ugh... Don't remind me" Her father winced

"Pops"

"Hmmm" He hummed

"What are you going to do with JJ? Momma said they arrested him"

Her father nodded, "Kill him is what I want to do. But probably not. I don't know, what do you want to do? I recommend locking the guy up for life"

"Psychiatric hospital"

"What?" Her father blinked

"He's crazy. He needs help, you can take him to court but I recommend psychiatric evaluation. And I don't want to be part of the trial. I don't want to see him"

"Of course. No one will subject you to that" he said holding her hands

"Pops"

"Hmm"

"What if I don't become a doctor"

"Why not?" he asked

"What if I don't go to university?"

"What's going on in that big brain of yours?" he asked, "Because you shouldn't be worried about whether or not you would get in. You should be worried about how many schools you'd have to pick from"

"I wrote my first JAMB when I was 14. I scored a 281. This year I scored a 312. Out of 400. They withheld my result for months! What do you think I would score next year?"

"400 out of 400?"

"Pop-pop!"

"What? I am proud of you. Can't I say that? "

"I don't want to be a doctor."

"What do you want to study then?" he asked her

"I'm 15. Most of the people in my class are 17. I feel like I've been running through my life too quickly and I just want to breathe finally"

"Those are good lyrics now"

"Haha" she said rolling her eyes.

"So what to you want to do? Travel? Take a vocational class? Anything you want to do is okay with me."

"You do know that other parents would have yelled at me by now right?"

"Mariah... I don't think you realize. You are a miracle. I was so dumb in school and your mother was a C average student. Her family weren't even able to send her to complete secondary school so she joined pageants. She got told about that she was beautiful and tall so she did the pageants to make money. The chances of both of us... Having someone as intelligent as you... Slim to none. But see... I trust you. And it has a lot to do with that fact that I'm pretty sure that you are smarter than me even as old as I am now. So... I trust. I worry for you... And you get me scared a lot but I trust you."

"I want to travel a bit. Help momma with the company. I really enjoy working with her."

"And that's not bad at all. See? Like I said smarted than me"

A knock on the door caused their attention to shift to the door. Mariah hadn't even noticed that it was almost four o'clock.

"Hey Mariah" He said

"Hi Harrison" she replied

"Good afternoon sir" Harrison said to her father.

"Pops, Harrison" Mariah said to her father.

"Harrison. Nice to meet you. You didn't come with Kami today I see" he noted

"She's on her way sir, I have somewhere to be and I just thought to drop by and see Mariah before I leave.

"That's okay." Her father said standing up "How tall are you?"

"POp-pop" Mariah rolled her eyes

"6'1. Last I checked sir"

"I'm leaving." he said raising his hands in the air. "I have to pick Sarah from the studio and bring her here anyways." he said heading for the door

"Bye pops" Mariah called after him and he waved her off. "Sit" she said and Harrison obliged her dropping his bag onto the tiled floor

"I'm sorry this happened Mariah. Are you okay?" Harrison asked

"Well my shoulder hurts badly and sometimes it feels like my head is going to split in two but asides that I'm good. How was the competition?"

"Mariah... Really?"

"Just tell me" she whined

"Fine" he said "We won"

"Are you lying to me?"

"We won, Mariah. We're going to Akwa Ibom for the Nationals in February"

"Why are you not happy about that?"

"Maybe because my girlfriend is in a hospital bed in pain and unable to walk"

"Don't forget that I'm seeing double"

"Mariah... " he whined

"I'm sorry. So what happened? How did Micah find me?"

"Well, her waited a while for you and I was starting to get worried since you only said you were going to get your bag. I told Micah. And he claimed we could do without you and that I should get into the bus and that he was going to get our allowance from the principal. The next thing I know he's yelling that we should call the ambulance and holding JJ by the throat so he could stop hitting you. It was pretty epic"

"I never knew Micah had feelings"

"Me neither. Did he come here? He left school pretty early I thought he was coming here."

Mariah shook her head. "What of Kami?" Mariah asked. She couldn't help it. Kami was her best friend and even if she was being a butch Mariah still loved her

"To be honest, she's been pretty down since... Well... You know. I haven't talked to her much though... She was here when I came in yesterday. She lingered by the door for a few hours and left."

Mariah talked to Harrison for a few more minutes and then he kissed her and left. He had to go to church with his parents that evening. Mariah sat in her bed bored out of her mind flicking through TV channels and Wishing that Christy hadn't left and neither had Harrison.

She hated hospitals.

Hard facts

"Who am I? Getting so many visitors today" Mariah commented as she saw Micah leaning against the door when she opened her eyes.

"Shut up your mouth. I wouldn't have pegged you for a fool Caiaphas but you surprised the hell out of me"

"Mr Micah" Mariah called sitting up"Thank you for coming"

He scratched his head. Walking up to her bed and shifting the chair closer as he walked.

"Don't thank me." he said waving his hands, "like I said your stupidity amazes me."

Mariah stared at him in confusion.

"Please. Don't act surprised... I knew you were scared of JJ. I've known for a while..."

"how?" Mariah asked

"Caiaphas do not insult me" Micah warned sternly "Recently you became happier. You cared less. You became more like a normal 16 year old. It wasn't hard to see the reason for the sudden change in your behaviour was Harrisonvs appearance. I'm not your father... But if you ask me, I'll take happy, smiling you over fake, plastic you any day. Now tell me why in God's name would you allow JJ treat you like thrash?"

Mariah gulped. "How..." she began unsure of what to say

"No. Don't give me that over used line that you didn't know. That's a bloody lie. You laid there and let him beat you up. Why? " Micah demanded

"I wanted someone to find me. For once, I wanted someone to find me" Mariah muttered under her breath

She wasn't sure that Micah had heard her initially, but he suddenly stilled in his movements and stared at her for a whole minute.

Then he did something she never had thought would happen in her entire life.

He hugged her.

Micah hugged her.

Mariah would have screamed if she wasn't the one currently being hugged by the most stone hearted teacher in her school. Her best teacher nonetheless.

"Nobody deserves to feel alone. nobody deserves to feel like that, Mariah. Trust me." he whispered against her hair. Mariah couldn't believe it, he called her by her first name. "OK. I'm leaving now. None of this sappy nonsense" He said finally releasing her and standing up.

"Mr Micah" Mariah called when he was almost at the door.

He spun around to face her humming

"You're my best teacher" she said.

He smiled, "You're the most intelligent student I've had in years, Mariah Caiaphas "

Mariah gasped. "I have to record this moment. You actually said it. Oh my God... Where is my phone.. "She squealed

"Oh shut up Caiaphas" he said and Mariah couldn't resist laughing.

"I heard you choked JJ... Didn't know you hid your muscles under the white shirts you wear daily"

"Your point is?"

"Thank you"

"My pleasure. I had fun doing it" he said and Mariah chuckled. "No really. Been looking for a reason to punch the dumbass"He said as he headed for the door.

"Also Abraham has been lurking around this corridor for two hours now. Take it easy on her she feels guilty enough. "

"What? Do you know everything now?" She joked

"Shut your smart-ass mouth, Mariah " he stated. One would have thought that he was annoyed. But the way he smiled when he said it, Mariah knew he wasn't.

He headed out of the doors"See you in school next week" Mariah called after him playfully. She'd be lucky if her parents let her out of her bed by the next week.

"I don't care" Micah called back and Mariah chuckled again.

Mariah shifted on her bed contemplating whether or not to talk to Kami. Finally giving in, she pressed the call button that was hanging beside her bed.

"Are you OK? " the nurse that came in asked her. It wasn't the nurse that had been assigned to her. So Mariah was surprised."I saw you press your call button and I assumed you needed help. I was just walking by."

That explained it. Mariah mused, her own nurse would never walk that quickly to see her.

"Do you need to go to the bathroom?" she asked again, "I know I'm not assigned to you but I promise you... I work here. I wouldn't try to kidnap you or anything."

"It's okay. I just wanted someone to help me call this girl." Mariah said lifting up her phone so the nurse could see it. The picture of her and Kami as her screen saver. "She should be outside"

"Okay. Not a problem" the nurse nodded and left the room.

Moments later Mariah lifted up her head to see Kami standing at the doorway.

"Come and Sit. And close the door" Mariah said Kami quietly did as she said.

"You been here for days now" Mariah stated.

"I'm sorry" Kami said quickly

"For what?"

"For saying all those things to Harrison. And for getting mad at you even when I had no reason to be. For not noticing that JJ was... You know?"

Mariah rolled her eyes "you didn't know or you didn't want to acknowledge it? Which is it?"

"I didn't know. Mariah there's no way I'd notice that and not do anything about it" Kami said

"You saw me cutting myself and did nothing about it" Mariah said more to herself than to Kami

"I'm sorry. Mariah. So sorry"

"That's not even what I'm mad at. You took something about me... That I told you as my best friend and you used it against me."

"I was angry at you"

"That's the part I cannot even comprehend. I know things, Kami. I know things about you. But no matter how mad I am, I would never breathe a word of it to anyone. And it's not even because we're friends. It's about being a decent human being."

"I'm sorry. I was just angry"

"that's what scares me the most" Mariah said, "So the next time we get in a argument what will you tell? Who would you tell?"

"Mariah, I swear I would never do it again"

"I don't believe you" Mariah said honestly

She felt bad when she saw Kami's face drop.

"Mariah" Kami called

"What do you want me to say?"

"That were still friends."

"You are still my friend Kami, but I can't say that I've forgiven you yet. I will. Eventually" Mariah said finally. She wasn't completely over what Kami did but she didn't want Kami to fell like she would never be forgiven.

Kami nodded. "Okay. I can live with that. Thank you"

It didn't matter how badly Mariah tried to hide it. Something was different. She wasn't sure if they'd ever be normal again and that was what scared her the most.

How do you like that chapter?. I'm many weeks late... I apologize. I'll try to be on time. This book is coming to an end and once it does just a little sugar will commence. I will be posting just a little sugar daily and The H.N.I.C weekly. Go over to my profile for the synopsis. Love alwaysMae

Soy sauce

Hopes were all I had

Dreams were all I got

No one as beautiful as you

Ever looked at me

The way you do

Mariah rolled her eyes for the umpteenth time that day as Harrison held his hands out to her. She ignored the gesture and propped her hands against the chasis of the car trying to stand up.

"Mariah let me help you" Harrison said but Mariah didn't hear him. He knew this. Her ears were plugged and she was listening to music. She had been since he told her they had to go home.Like she was mad at himHe held the door of the passenger's seat open for her, but he kept his hands to himself.

She stumbled and he held unto he arms steadying her. She didn't struggle, he was glad, instead she rested her weight on his body.Harrison slowly helped her into the car and she sighed when she was finally seated. Shutting

the door he folded up the wheelchair and placed it in the boot of the car
then he turned round to the driver seat.

"Mariah" Harrison called as he turned on the ignition.

Mariah ignored him. He backed out of the parking space and into the
street, slowly.

"Mariah your mum said I should bring you home, that's not my fault"
Harrison tried again. Mariah wasn't having it though. She hated being
treated like she was handicapped even though technically she was.

She turned up the volume of her earphones. It wasn't his fault, she knew.
But she couldn't help it. She was annoyed and frustrated, so she ignored
him.

This girl

This girl...

With her eyes like pools of melted chocolate

On me

It has to be miracle

Highly unusual

Has to be a miracle

Chocolate eyes

Love someone like me

She looked up to see Harrison staring at he r like he was waiting for her to
give a reply to a question she had asked.

"What?" she snapped

"I asked if you wanted to watch a movie or eat something before we head home" Harrison asked again.

"Whatever" Mariah murmured plugging her earphones back in her ears

Harrison sighed. Physiotherapy hadn't been going so well for Mariah for the past few weeks. She got frustrated because of it. It made Harrison sad, seeing her struggle. He couldn't imagine what she was feeling, going from being able to walk to not being able to could fuck anybody up.

If it's a dream I hope I never wake up

They say love is blind

But I hope you can see the real me

It has to be a miracle

Purely a miracle

Highly unusual

that you love me

The way that you do

It has to a miracle

It's highly unusual

It's gotta be a miracle

Chocolate eyes love someone like me

Harrison pulled up in front of chicken Republic. It was the closest place he could get food before heading to Mariah's home to drop her off.

He pulled out the earplugs from her ears as he pointed towards the building opposite them.

"What the hell did you do that for?" She yelled.

"Let's go" He said ignoring her outburst

"I'm not going anywhere with you" she said

"Mariah. C'mon" he pleaded, "Let's just get food then I'll take you home"

Mariah hissed "You want to take me... in a wheel chair... Into chicken Republic. Do you like being pitied or something? Let's just go home"

Harrison ignored her he got out of the car and headed inside. It didn't take him more than ten minutes. He got his food and was back outside again, walking towards the car. He handed one pack to Mariah when he got in to the car. She spend up the bag and basically stuck her head inside.

"I got you lemonade. Wilsons lemonade. I know you don't like any other type." He said starting up the car again

"Thanks " she whispered. Harrison wouldn't have heard it if he wasn't looking at her at the time

"There's no soy sauce" he continued, "I know you hate that"

Mariah nodded peeking in the bag again.

Harrison glanced at her multiple times as he drove.

"What?" she asked him

Harrison shrugged in response. "Nothing. I love you"
"Huh?"

"I'm in love with you" he repeated

Mariah sucked in a breath in between her teeth, making a small 'tch' sound. "You are so corny"

"I am" Harrison said glancing at her once again

"Hello? Sir? Watch the road please... you just barely got your licence" Mariah chided

"Ah look at that." Harrison hummed, "My real girlfriend is back"

Mariah rolled her eyes and shook her head and Harrison chuckled. Soon enough the Car was filled with their laughter. They were laughing at absolutely nothing, but they both loved it.

"I'm sorry I act so annoyingly sometimes" she said

"Annoyingly? " he asked his brows furrowing

Mariah sucked her teeth again, "Don't bother my English language" she chided, "What I'm saying is I'm sorry. I'm just..."

"I get it" Harrison said cutting her off, "Somewhat." He continued as he slowed the car to a stop, in front of traffic light that had just turned red "life dealt you a bad hand and it's okay if you want to scream. I'm not going to judge you for that. You can yell at me all you want"

Mariah nodded. She wanted to say she loved him and she wanted to thank him for always helping and always understanding, but she couldn't find that words. So she kept her mouth shut like her tongue was tied and she stared at him, like he'd be able to read her expression, like he'd be able to read the fact that she loved him off her face.

The light turned green and he moved the car again, branching off onto the right. The road that Mariah was sure would lead right to her house.

"Can we stop for a moment?" Mariah asked, "I want to eat before I get home"

Harrison wordlessly parked by the side of the road beside a sign board that read Mutual Alliance.An insurance company, he read that much off the board.

"Mariah," he called, "Why don't you want to go home?"

Mariah shrugged "Nothing. I miss you and school and I just don't want to be home right now" Harrison stared at her skeptical, "My parents treat me like I'm handicapped!" She added exasperated, reaching for the bag containing her meal

"And I don't? " was Harrison' s only reply. He watched as Mariah opened up the paper plate and bit into the fish first. She was of the opinion that if your fish wasn't cooked well then your food would be wack too. Harrison smiled inwardly at the thought.

"No. You try to help but you know when to let me be and when to step in and help"

Harrison smiled, "Okay. 10 minutes. Then I take you home" he said, "Your , other might soon start calling me" he murmured under his breath as he took out his own plate "if you are tired of being around mere mortals like us you can come to the house and have an huge conversation with Manny." He added.

They ate, not in total silence, Mariah commented on people that passed by them, guessing their ages and which ones had better clothes. Harrison smiled fondly at her and gave his input once in a while.

He was done with his meal before her and he sipped on his water while he waited for Mariah to finish up her lemonade.

"Are you going to come back to school? " He asked as she wiped her lips with a paper towel.

She shrugged. "Maybe. Maybe not. I wrote all the exams last year, so there's really no need for me to come back to school."Harrison sighed"Have you decided on what uni you're going to?" Mariah asked him

"Unilag?" He said almost unsure. "Unilag" he said again, "You? "

"Unilag"

"Why?"

"What do you mean why? You just said that's where you're going"

"So you want to go where I'm going? Why? You have the opportunity to go anywhere you why would you chose unilag why would you even choose Nigeria? "

"So you think I'm crazy because I want us to go to the same school? "

"Mariah I want to go to the same school with you. But we are from vastly different backgrounds. You can afford to go to better schools, I can't. My mother works in Unilag so I'll probably get some form of discount. My dad is a soldier and as much as I would like to believe that nigeria pays their soldiers well we both know that not the case."

"My parents didn't go to university..." she began

"It doesn't matter. You should aim to be better than them"

"You cannot limit yourself to just lagos, you are a very intelligent person" Mariah said, "You could get a scholarship"

"Mariah..." He began to argue

"Just try it." She countered holding his hands. "Where do you really want to go?" She asked.

"Unilag" he replied like an answering machine

"Are you lying to me?" She asked

"New York" he began, "I've been looking at school's there for years. Since I was 15 I think"

Mariah smiled, "Let's try that, you're writing the exams next month, you do well in those I think you might be eligible to apply for a scholarship"

"Where do you really want to go?" He asked her

"Wharton" she replied quite easily, "I don't mind going to Wharton for post graduate though."

He shook his head, "Mm mmh" he hummed leaning in to kiss her. She chuckled as she held the sides of his face.

"What?" He asked smiling a bit

"Soy sauce. You taste like soy sauce" she said as she kissed him again.

Do settlements annoy you?

Mariah hadn't been to her therapist's office in weeks. She had skipped out of most of her sessions willingly -her parents did not approve of- and the ones she hadn't skipped out of she was forced to have at her home. Just like today, as she lay on the sofa staring at the ceiling of her father's study. Her therapist stared at her, her eyes willing Mariah to speak. Still, Mariah stared at the ceiling silently. As if the criss cross semi metallic designs drawn on them were the most interesting things ever.

"Mariah. I..." the therapist began but Mariah opened her mouth cutting her off

"Nice shoes" Mariah hummed her eyes never leaving the ceiling

"Thank you" she replied, and after another moment of silence she asked, "what's on your mind, Mariah"

Mariah sighed "Am I naive for wishing that he'd get a more serious pun-ishment than a settlement

"Mariah, I think settlement is pretty severe"

"I've had two surgeries on my leg..." Mariah said and it's still pretty useless"

"Mariah physiotherapy takes time" the therapist said, "you've only been at it for a few weeks anyways"

"But still 10 million..."

"Does the settlement annoy you, Mariah?"

"He probably won't even get to see a psychiatrist"

"Your father says he will be compelled to, It was one of the terms of the agreement"

Mariah nodded, "but he can forge it right?"

"I don't think he would do that" she replied

Mariah nodded.

"How is Kami?" The therapist asked. Mariah turned to look at her for a quick second

"I don't know" she said as she went back to staring at the ceiling.

"Why haven't you spoken to her?" She asked

"It's not that I don't want to talk to her, I just don't know what to say to her. And she's not going to talk to me either so...."

"Maybe she feels guilty"

"She does." Mariah replied

"But do you blame her?"

"For what happened with JJ? No" Mariah replied, "I mean I thought she knew and didn't do anything about it but I didn't blame her. I don't blame her"

"Have you told her that? "

"No. Should I have told her?"

"Maybe" The therapist shrugged, "Do you want to be friends with Kami again?"

Mariah shrugged "Maybe" and her doctor laughed

Harrison was, as Mariah was trying hard to speak to her therapist again, trying to tell his dad that his father wanted to meet him.

"Daddy can I tell you something" Harrison asked as he pushed the ludo board to the side and began packing up the players and dice.

"Yes" his dad replied pushing himself forward on his seat and linking his fingers together. "What is it?"

"My father," Harrisin began "he wants to meet me"

"I know"

"You know?"

"I do" his dad nodded, "Your mum told me"

"Do you think he has changed?" Harrison asked

His father shook his head, "I don't know the newer to that question" his father replied

Harrison sighed, "Well do you think I should go?"

His father shook his head, "I cannot tell you that"

Harrison groaned, "Why?"

"Because he is your father"

"But he doesn't do half the things that you do for me. In fact he doesn't do anything for me. Except try to burn me alive apparently" Harrison said, murmuring the last part under his breath.

Suprisingly his father chuckled, "Do you remember when I started seeing your mother?" He asked

Harrison nodded wordlessly. How could he forget, the tall imposing man that he'd thought had come to get him for not picking up his plate after eating. He remembered his mother telling him that the man was her friend and that they were going to be spending more time together. Harrison didn't understand it much but the next thing he knew there was a wedding and then he had had a little brother.

"You were six or seven at the time" his father smiled, "You were eating an Oreo. It was your oreo phase" Harrison nodded, he remembered. He had gone through a phase where he'd eat no other biscuits other that oreos."and I asked you what you had in your hand and the cut the cookie into two and handed one to me"

"And you said no. You said you didn't like oreos" Harrison completed rolling his eyes. Like he couldn't understand who would not eat oreos.

"Yes and your eyes, the were just so large. Like your tiny brain couldn't comprehend how somebody could not like chocolate" he chuckled

"I still don't. I mean I shared my precious Oreo with you and you said no" Harrison said smiling

"Do you remember what you said to me that day?" His dad asked

Harrison shook his head, asides the Oreo debacle, he had no further memories of that day.

"You asked me if I came to get you. And when I said no you said I shouldn't let them get you. That boy I saw that day, afraid, I'd do anything for that boy. You're a great son Harrison, and I don't pay your fees because I'm married to your mother, I pay it because you're my son. You are my son and a father should take care of his children. So see your father if you want to, I'll always be here. 'Kay?" His dad hummed

Harrison had to blink to prevent the tears that were building up behind his eyes from falling forward. He shook his head. Once. Twice.

"What? " his dad asked

"I'm not going to see him" Harrison replied

"That's fine" his father smiled. "How's Mariah doing?" He asked and Harrison groaned

"What?" His father inquired

"Nothing."

"Okay since you're not going to tell me," His father said placing his hand on his knees and getting up, "I'm going to the gym"

"Wait. Daddy wait"

"Mm mmh" he shook his head as he ascended the narrow stairs, "the time has passed boy"

"Can I come to the gym with you?" Harrison asked following his father up the stairs

"So that you can tear Bako's muscle again at wrestling and 'accidently' bump Nedu into the beam again?"

"Don't use air quotes it was an accident"

"I believe you Harrison" his father said, his voice laced with sacarsm.

"Then why didn't you say anything when he came to talk to you about it? Why did you agree with me if you didn't believe me?" Harrison asked they were now standing in front of his parents' room.

"You think I'll take someone's side over my child's? And in public?"

Harrison smiled, then he went back to begging, "Please... i promise I won't accidentally hit Nedu in the face. Even if he says stupid shit"

His father nodded."I'll be in the car in five minutes"

He didn't even need to finish his statement, Harrison was prancing off to change into his sports gear.

"And if you do manage to punch Nedu this week, " his father called out to him, "at least do it properly. I didn't teach you to box for show"

Harrison smiled at the thought. Maybe some day he'd have two dad's but right now, he was content with the one he had.

Pre and post Jesus

- -

D ecember 2018

The difference between Harrison's church and the one her parents used to go to on Christmas day was that she actually enjoyed this one. Whilst the latter was long winded and sleep inducing, Harrison's was fun.

Fun.

Words she never thought she'd use in describing a church service. The members danced more that they did at parties she went to.The choir sang a good song that a ton of people in the congregation seemed to know. The pastor was funny. Funny and made sense in a way.

Love everyone.

God is love.

It didn't really make sense in her head but the people he was talking to seemed to get it.

At the end of the message she decided that she liked Jesus.

He seemed liked a cool guy.

"Mariah"

She turned around.

"What are you going to have?" Harrison asked her.

They were seated at a large table at the Home Kitchen. An upscale restuarant in the mainland of the town.

She saw that they were all waiting Forget to say something. She looked at the menu that Harrison had slipped in front of her without her knowledge.

"Egusi and poundo" she said slowly.

Harrison's mother nodded and procedded to repeat what she had said to the waiter.

"Hey" Harrison said. He was smiling at her. She hated that. She'd given Harrison so much grief over the past couple of weeks and he was still nice to her. He still treated her well. He smiled at her all the time. She didn't like comparing him to JJ..but her subconscious mind did.

Mariah hadn't seen JJ since she woke up at the hospital. Her father threatened fire and brimstone on him and his family but the case was settled outside of court. Mariah hated that. She wanted JJ to have a court ordered psychiatric evaluation, that had been one of the terms of the settlement, somehow she wasn't sure that part of the agreement would be carried out.

Harrison nudged her again. "what's going on in that head?" he asked

She shouldn't be ignoring Harrison. Why was she here with the family in Christmas day? Because Harrison shared the same birthday with Jesus.

"I'm here." she mumbled.

Harrison chuckled."I can see that. Are you okay?"

Mariah nodded. "mmhmm" she hummed.

Aretha was seated on her father's lap on the opposite side of the table trying to eat banana slices that had been placed in a plate in front of her. Trying to. Somehow the slices kept getting stuck in between her fingers and falling back into the plate. Her dad helped and eventually she got about three slices in her mouth at the same time. Her cheeks were puffed up and it made Mariah chuckle.

"mawiah bwing the ammama" she said her cheeks full.

Mariah didn't know how she had been able to decipher what the 2year old was saying because even her father had patted her back and asked her to finish chewing.

"The camera is in my bag. We'll take pictures later" Mariah said.

Aretha nodded turning around to face her father. She reached for his shirt and he shook his head. The banana juices would only end up leaving a stain on this shirt.

"Picture. Daddy. Picture"

"Yes 'Retha we'd take pictures later." her father replied.

"I think your mother hates me" Mariah whispered

"She doesn't. Why would you say that? " Harrison asked

"She never smiles at me"

"She thinks we're having sex"

"Are we having sex?"

"Are you asking me?"

"Yes... "

"Mariah... "

"Like are we supposed to be having sex. Is that something we should be doing...?

"Keep talking like you think I don't know what sex is." Manny said from beside Harrison.

"Shut up! No body was talking to you here" Harrison chided as quietly as he could.

"Yeah. You're doing a pretty terrible job of not involving the whole table in your sex discussion" Manny said

"Manny! " Harrison yelled smacking that back of his head.

"Ow!"

"Harrison. Don't hit your brother!"

"You don't know what he said to me" Harrison replied

"I don't care"

"Tell her what I sad" Manny challenged

"What did you say, Manny"

Harrison eyeballed him"Nothing, mummy. I said nothing. "

Mariah chuckled, rolling her eyes at the playfulness of the two brothers.

"Are you excited about this birthday?" you're 18 today."

"Not as much as I'm excited to be done with school."

"Secondary school "

"Still. I'm happy"

"So are you writing JAMB with us mere mortals?"

"No."

"But if you were, what course would you write for?"

"Business. Have you decided your course"

"Nope. No idea"

"You could go to New York and study food. "

"I can't go to New York, Mariah. I have to be realistic. "

Mariah rolled her eyes. "if you had the funds would you go?"

"They haven't even offered me the admission yet. "

"Harry stop berating yourself, you mango"

"Fine. If I get the admission and I have the funds, yes I would go"

"Good. My father wants to give you a scholarship."

"Stop it"

"I told him about you and he wants to pay for you"

"Mariah!" he yelled. The whole table was staring at them now, "Why would you do that?!"

"Why are you yelling? Are you a mad person" his mother said. His father just shook his head disappointedly at him, still trying to clean banana juices from between her fingers.

Their food had arrived and Mariah was staring at the colourful Egusi soup and she couldn't see it. Her vision was blurry. Why is Harrison telling at her? Why is Harry shouting at her? Why is Harry shouting at her?

Why is H... JJ shouting at her? What is JJ doing here?

Harrison cursed as he watched as Mariah stilled in her seat. "I'm sorry" he mumbled over and over again. "I'm sorry. I'm sorry"

"Mariah. Mariah" his dad called, " what's the other guy's name"

"What?"

"The other guy. The one that uhmmm.."

"oh... JJ

"Mariah listen to me. Harrison is not JJ. Okay? Harrison is not JJ. Say something to her"

"it's me Mariah. It's Harrison. I'm sorry for yelling " He said squeezing her hand

Mariah finally nodded opening her eyes.

"Are you okay?" Harrison's father asked

"I'm fine" She replied

"She's obviously not fine" Harrison argued.

"She says she's fine. She's fine" his dad said.

"I'm sorry" Harrison said again.

"She's going to have flashbacks often. That's very normal for someone who has been through a traumatic experience. Just let her know you're not JJ. And be patient"

Harrison's mother was eerily silent and so was Manny. Like they couldn't believe how much the incident had affected Mariah's life.

"Stop staring at her like that, she's going to therapy. Twice a week now"Harrison chided his brother and maybe his mother a little.

Aretha the only one seemingly unbothered by the unexpected turn of events reached out and wiped the tears that was on Mariah's cheek. A tear that Mariah didn't even know was there. Her fingers were still sticky from the banana slices. But Mariah couldn't resist smiling.

"Mawiah sorry" Aretha said waving at her.

"Do you want to give her a hug? " her dad asked and Aretha nodded.

Aretha moved on to Mariah's lap and wrapped her arms around Mariah's neck.

Mariah held her. "When daddy goes to work and I'm sad. Awison say I can cry too. Awison say crying is good. And when I cry Awison hugs me tight. You can cry too Mawiah, I will hug you tight."

Mariah chuckled tears welling up in her eyes. How can a two year old be so sensitive? Whoever they were training this girl to be, she'd be such an amazing human.

She liked this family... She loved Harrison, Aretha was beautifulManny was smartTheir mother was overly protective

Mariah stared at Harrison's dad. Was he Jesus? She liked Jesus. He's a cool dude.

THE END